Cross Connection

Jugal Hansraj is a feature film actor, writer and a National Award-winning film director based in Mumbai. He began working in films first as a child actor—*Masoom* (1983)—and went on to become a lead actor in films like *Papa Kahte Hai* (1996) and *Mohabbatein* (2000). In 2006, he turned writer-director and made the animated film *Roadside Romeo* and in 2010 he directed the feature film *Pyaar Impossible!* He is currently the Head of Creative Development for new projects at Dharma Productions. *Cross Connection* is his first book.

Shrirang Sathaye has been an animation-lover, designer and director for thirty years. He currently works as an animation consultant. His other interests include political/satirical cartoons and illustrations.

Cross Connection
The Big Circus Adventure

JUGAL HANSRAJ

Illustrations by
SHRIRANG SATHAYE

Published in Red Turtle by
Rupa Publications India Pvt. Ltd 2018
7/16, Ansari Road, Daryaganj New Delhi 110002

Sales Centres:
Allahabad Bengaluru Chennai
Hyderabad Jaipur Kathmandu
Kolkata Mumbai

Copyright © Jugal Hansraj 2018

Illustrations by Shrirang Sathaye 2018

This is a work of fiction. Names, characters,
places and incidents are either the product of the author's imagination or are
used fictitiously and any resemblance to any actual person,
living or dead, events or locales is entirely coincidental.
All rights reserved.

No part of this publication may be reproduced, transmitted,
or stored in a retrieval system, in any form or by any means,
electronic, mechanical, photocopying, recording or otherwise,
without the prior permission of the publisher.

ISBN: 978-81-291-4958-9

First impression 2018

10 9 8 7 6 5 4 3 2 1

The moral right of the author has been asserted.

Printed by Excel Printers Pvt. Ltd., New Delhi

This book is sold subject to the condition that it shall not,
by way of trade or otherwise, be lent, resold, hired out,
or otherwise circulated, without the publisher's prior consent,
in any form of binding or cover other than that in which it is published.

*To my father, who always encouraged creativity,
my mother, wife Jasmine and brother Sunil for being
my support system.
And my mentor Dr Daisaku Ikeda,
President Soka Gakkai International.*

Chapter 1

'It sure is good to be back home!' Said Uncle Geri to no one in particular as he took a deep breath and let the crisp and clear mountain air fill his lungs. He adjusted his spectacles and looked up at the sky, which was just starting to turn a light shade of pink. He had enjoyed his last few weeks with his brothers and sisters and their families who lived in the plains. But he was now back where he belonged. He smiled as he sprung from his perch and took flight.

Oops! I'm sorry, dear reader—I think I'm getting ahead of myself here. You must be wondering what this is all about. Let me backtrack a little bit and introduce you to Uncle Geri and where we are in the story, so that there is no confusion. As a wise old man (don't ask me who, I've forgotten now) once said, 'Let's begin at the beginning!'

Our story begins in the outskirts of a charming little hill station called Kamalpur, nestled in the towering Himalayas in North India. Though it was towards the end of the winter season, the mountains still had their snowcaps on. Perched atop one of the higher branches of a big, beautiful green oak tree was the wise old bluebird—Mr Geri Atric, known to his friends simply as Uncle Geri. Well, the green oak tree wasn't very green as it was still winter. But anyway...

Uncle Geri lived in the most interesting place—a place no child (bird or human alike) could resist—The Great Indian Circus! Though currently stationed outside Kamalpur, the circus travelled to the nearby hill stations as the seasons changed. Uncle Geri didn't really perform at the circus but had lived there for as long as he could remember and all the animals there were his best friends. They looked up to him for all sorts of advice and it would be safe to say that it was Uncle Geri who pretty much kept all things under control. Of course, the person with complete control of the circus was Mr Gulshan Circuswala, the lovable chubby human, who not only owned it but also treated all the animals there with a lot of love—like they were his own children. And they in turn loved him back and wanted to make him proud. All the animals were housed in separate enclosures and all of them roamed freely around the circus. None of them were caged. They loved being part of the Great Indian Circus. Children and grown-ups from all over would come to this town to see the circus animals perform and go back home happy.

Gliding through the cold wintry breeze, The Great Indian Circus came into view. The old bluebird dove down over the circus gates just as children and elders alike were eagerly walking through the gates, waiting to see their favourite animals perform. Candy floss, popcorn and other snacks were being sold and everyone had a big smile on their faces. Uncle Geri turned to the huge circus tent that almost looked like candy itself—white with broad red stripes. As he glided over the entrance, the gatekeeper, though busy checking tickets, gave a quick smile to Uncle Geri as he flew into the big tent.

It was a full house! Uncle Geri soared above the audiences who were taking their seats. The circus tent was indeed huge—almost as big as a stadium! The circus jokers were keeping the

audiences entertained as they took their seats. The old bluebird flew to the other side, from where all the performers made their grand entrance. Behind it was the backstage where they all warmed up and waited for their turn to go onstage. Uncle Geri was excited! He couldn't wait to say hello to all those big animals—again!

He flew through the backstage and landed on top of a big ladder, which was leaning against the tent outside. Right before him were his two favourites. The two most magnificent and imposing creatures he had ever known—Bhole Ram the Brave and Savitri, of course.

Bhole Ram, the big grey elephant, was the star attraction of the circus and part of the famous opening act. Although he looked imposing, he was probably the most soft-hearted and shy animal in the troupe—you could say he was a gentle giant! And right beside him was his partner in the opening act, the massive, beautiful and equally gentle female elephant Savitri, who was busy warming up with the big, round beach ball in front of her. And Bhole was...well, Bhole Ram was as usual looking at Savitri, transfixed by her beautiful big round eyes! Poor chap...this Bhole. What with him being crazily in love with Savitri and all. In spite of his size and bravery, when it came to talking to Savitri, his words would come out all higgledy-piggledy. He would be like a nervous little chicken every time he came close to Savitri, which was every day. Anyway, remind me to tell you more about this love story (or the lack of it) later.

Both the elephants looked up at Uncle Geri and smiled. They said their hellos with a great deal of excitement!

'Uncle Geri! Welcome back! We missed you!'

Just then there was a loud roar. Now hang on, the lion hasn't entered the story yet. That roar was a loud roar...of applause! The opening act with Bhole Ram and Savitri had been announced and the crowd went wild with anticipation. The two elephants waved their trunks at Uncle Geri and in they went, to perform their signature 'Balancing on Beach Ball' act.

Uncle Geri looked on proudly as the two elephants expertly did their balancing act set to music. The crowds went wild, but that was only expected. The opening act received a standing ovation and loud cheers as the elephants made their exits.

'Udi Baba! Oncle Geri Dada!'

Uncle Geri smiled when he heard his name being called out that way. That was Pintu—or as he was affectionately known to all: Pintu Da—the Royal Bengal tiger. Uncle Geri turned back to see the greasy black hair, neatly parted in the middle, on top of a big tiger head. Pintu Da was a classical singer! He was an attraction in his own right. Though the annoying part about his singing abilities was that he kept singing even when he wasn't on stage. To be honest, it did get a little irritating, but who would mind it when Pintu himself was so loveable! Pintu Da laughed with glee—he was happy to see Uncle Geri and had so much to catch up on but it would have to wait. Duty called.

'See you soooo-oooo-oooooon,' sang Pintu Da as he made his way to the stage amidst loud cheering.

Uncle Geri surely lived in the coolest place ever! As he heard a familiar nervous shuffle behind him, he could feel his laughter climbing up through his little belly and struggling to come out of his mouth in a loud burst, but he suppressed it. He had to be polite. Right in front of him, hesitatingly and nervously shuffling up towards the entrance of the tent was the majestic-looking king of beasts: Chintamani the Lion! His shiny, wavy mane was fluttering regally in the breeze.

You might be wondering why Uncle Geri felt like laughing on seeing this most majestic of animals? Have no worry, I'll explain. You see, this big lion, though he looked majestic, deep in his heart he was just a little scaredy cat! As Uncle Geri was struggling to hold back his laughter and say hello, Chintamani spoke up. Well, spoke is a more relative term. Let's say he shrilled, for his voice was a high-pitched shrill unlike any lion you've ever heard. He looked like a majestic lion but spoke like a little schoolgirl! His voice just didn't match up to other lions. And that's not all. He was a nervous, shrinking violet, scared about almost anything and everything—he even had stage fright! But all the other animals adored him. He was a sweetheart after all.

'H-h-hello U-Uncle Geri...' said Chintamani timidly.

The old bluebird was indeed delighted to see his anxiety-ridden friend again! He gestured a thumbs up to wish the lion all the best! Just then, Mr Gulshan ran up to Chintamani and goaded him lovingly. Feeling better, the lion nervously walked on to the stage to loud cheering.

'Ladies and gentlemen...boys and girls... please welcome the one and only...the pride of this circus...the ferocious king of the jungle... Chintamani the Lion!'

The kids jumped up in joy as the king of the jungle strode in trying his best to look confident. He looked back at Mr Gulshan, who nodded. Chintamani stopped and opened his mouth to roar, and that very moment Mr Gulshan turned on the sound system where a pre-recorded ferocious lion roar played on the loudspeakers. Chintamani mimed it perfectly and the crowd loved it!

Every time Chintamani walked on stage, the audience expected him to roar loudly, just like a lion would. But you and I know his secret. So, Mr Gulshan devised a plan to play a lion's roar on the sound system and our Chintamani would just mime to it. A star was born!

Uncle Geri looked around for the little monkey who was the favourite of all the children in the audience. They loved his tricks up on the trapeze. But he was nowhere to be seen.

'Where is Chunky?' thought Uncle Geri. 'I wonder what mischief he might be up to...'

Chapter 2

'Ladies and gentlemen...boys and girls...you will now see the king of beasts...the majestic Chintamani run and jump through that big, round hoop of fire!'

There was a flutter of excitement in the audience. Chintamani took a deep breath and tried to pay no attention to the bead of sweat starting to form on his brow. He had done this with ease numerous times, but he would still feel butterflies in his tummy before making the jump. He looked towards the backstage at Mr Gulshan who gave him a big encouraging smile. It made him feel a bit better. What he didn't notice though, was a pair of eyes looking at him from behind an old wooden chest which was just by the stage entrance. Those eyes—let me rephrase that—those very mischievous eyes belonged to a very mischievous monkey. In his hands he carried a slingshot, and in that slingshot was a fat, round stone. The little monkey closed one eye to take aim. His target? Chintamani's buttocks! Just as he pulled back the slingshot, there was a shuffle behind him and the slingshot was whacked out of his hand!

'Chunky!'

The monkey had to crane his neck really far back to see the source of the booming voice. His worst fears were confirmed. It was Bhole Ram, looking very annoyed! Chunky took a deep breath and readied himself for the boring lecture that was about to begin.

'Chunky! Here you go again trying to play pranks and disrupting everything and everybody!'

Chunky rolled his eyes and muttered, 'Here we go again...what a bore!'

'What was that?' Asked Bhole Ram, getting even more agitated.

'Nothing!' Chunky lied.

The lecture, which Chunky pretty much knew by heart now, continued.

'Why are you always up to no good? That poor Chintamani is terrified of something going wrong during his performance. Why do you keep bullying him so? Get out of here right now and practice your trapeze act or else I will teach you such a lesson that you will forget your own name!'

Chunky stood up, rubbing the dust off his body. 'Bhole! Just chill buddy! Why can't a monkey just have some innocent fun?'

'The name is Bhole Ram! Not Bhole! And fun? You call ruining somebody's performance fun? Especially someone with a nervous disposition like Chintamani?'

Back on the centre stage in the big tent a drum roll began. It was the build up to Chintamani's jump through the hoop.

Chunky hopped up onto the wooden chest and tried to reason with Bhole Ram. 'But lions aren't supposed to be nervous! Instead of being ferocious like the rest of his tribe, Chintu is the most nervous creature I have ever seen!'

Bhole Ram, losing his patience, lifted Chunky up onto his massive trunk. 'His name is Chintamani—he hates being called Chintu! Try and understand, it ruins his reputation as a lion! And nervous or not, that doesn't give you any reason to trouble anyone, least of all him. And I'm pretty sure now that all the pranks that have been played in the last few days have been your doing, only I can't prove it!'

Chunky raised his eyebrows and drawled, 'Booooring!'

'I heard that!'

There was no getting past Bhole Ram who always lectured Chunky like a strict schoolteacher. With Chunky on his trunk, Bhole Ram decided to just take him away from the place before he could do any harm. As Bhole Ram turned to walk away, Chunky noticed the slingshot and the fat round stone that had fallen by the wayside. In a flash, he swooped down and picked them up. Bhole Ram was slowly walking away when Chunky turned around to face the stage and took aim. The drum roll on the stage had gotten louder and Chintamani was starting his run up. The crowd cheered for him. No sooner did he get to his mark from where he was to take the big leap, than Chunky let loose the fat stone from the slingshot. It cut through the air just as Chintamani's hind legs took off from the ground and BAM! The stone found its target. Chunky rarely ever missed. So, instead of flying through the loop, Chintamani screamed and fell in a heap on the first few rows of the audience.

Now, imagine if a big strong lion fell in your lap! There was pandemonium all around as the crowd ran helter-skelter in a state of panic. Backstage, Mr Gulshan slapped his head in frustration. Bhole Ram turned to see what the commotion was about.

'OOOOWWW! I've been hit...on the butt!' wailed Chintamani.

But of course the panicking crowd of humans didn't understand his language and for them it sounded like the lion was roaring (well, wailing actually). They panicked even more.

Bhole Ram looked down questioningly at

Chunky who was still perched on his trunk, wearing his most innocent 'who, me?' expression.

'Dude! Don't look at me like that! I've been on your trunk this whole time—I had nothing to do with that clumsy Chintu falling all over the place!'

Uncle Geri, who had just flown back moments before the mishap, flapped his wings close to Bhole Ram's ear and said, 'He did it! I saw Chunky shooting that slingshot from your trunk when you were walking away!'

Bhole Ram was livid. He looked down at his trunk but there was no one there.

Chunky, once again, had gotten away!

From behind a pile of hay, Chunky peeked at Bhole Ram scratching his head with his trunk wondering where the little monkey had run off. A big, naughty smirk found its way on Chunky's face. He muttered to himself, 'They don't call me Chunky the Funky monkey for nothing!'

Night had fallen. Bhole Ram, with Uncle Geri hovering near his ear, started walking towards the elephant enclosure when he noticed Savitri passing by. He let out a deep sigh of longing. On noticing the two, she walked up to them.

'Hello again!' She greeted them with her sweet smile. Bhole Ram, as usual, got flustered with excitement.

'Uh...huh...hmmm...er...'

Savitri smiled again and there was an awkward pause. Uncle Geri stepped in to save the day.

'Hello Savitri! Ha-ha don't mind Bhole Ram... he's just a bit agitated with all that's been happening!'

She smiled at Bhole Ram understandingly, 'I heard! I do hope Chintamani is okay.'

'Uh...huh...hmmm...er...'

Uncle Geri had to speak up again, 'The poor lion! His anxiety must have gone through the roof! That Chunky and his tricks!'

Savitri nodded in agreement, 'Well he is a naughty little fellow! Anyway, I'll see you around.'

'Uh...huh...hmmm...er...'

Savitri walked away. Bhole Ram let out a deep sigh.

'I just love talking to her!'

Uncle Geri flapped his wings in frustration.

'You'll love talking to her when you actually do! When will you ever muster up the courage to tell her that your fat heart goes BOOM BOOM every time you see her?'

'There has to be a right moment, Uncle Geri!'

'Right moment, my left wing! You've known her for such a long time and yet you can't even speak to her. Next time, I'll push you for it!'

Bhole Ram took another deep breath and turned to walk towards the elephant enclosure. Uncle Geri looked at him walking away and thought to himself,

'And they call you Bhole Ram the Brave. Brave at everything except this!'

Chapter 3

'WAAAAAAAAAAAA!' Chintamani continued wailing as Mr Gulshan gently prodded him on towards the lion enclosure and tried his best to perk up his spirits.

'It's fine...you did very well...it's not your fault at all. Don't you worry about a thing.'

'WAAAAAAAAAAAA!'

Clearly this perking up thing wasn't working. As they continued walking, they passed a shaded area in a part of the circus that wasn't being used anymore and which had some old cages at the far back. One big cage had some shadows moving about.

A shadow from the back of the cage moved closer to the cage bars. But it was not actually a shadow...it was a shadowy looking big black panther. As he walked to the front of the cage, a shaft of light caught his face and his pupils contracted, making him look even more menacing. His eyes followed Mr Gulshan as he

led Chintamani away. At the back of the cage something moved. Four more shadowy figures walked up to its front where the light fell on their faces to reveal four more panthers. One of them walked up to the panther in the front and growled, 'Boss, did you see that? That good-for-nothing Gulshan gives so much importance to those foolish animals...'

The panther in the front was Kaalia, the leader of the gang and black as night. He grunted menacingly and growled in a low-pitched deep, gruff, grating voice, 'That would have never happened if I was allowed to roam free instead of those fools. Not even a leaf would flutter without my permission. Gulshan has locked us here to discipline us...Ha! I'll teach him a thing or two about discipline!'

You must be wondering why indeed Mr Gulshan locked these panthers up. I had said that he was a sweet chubby human who loved all these animals like his own children. Well, I said that because it is true! Mr Gulshan did love all the animals in the circus, including the five panthers. But they had started to get out of control. There was an incident some months ago when the panthers, led by Kaalia, had pounced on the audience for jeering at them for being mean to the other animals that were performing. Luckily, no one was hurt. The authorities came to the circus the next day to order Mr Gulshan to hand over the panthers to them. But he always believed in the good in every living creature, even if they behaved mean at the time. He managed to seek permission to keep them as long as they didn't come before the audiences again. This way Mr Gulshan got to keep them at the circus but on the insistence of the authorities and for the safety of the others, he had to keep them locked in a big cage. He secretly hoped that they would realize their mistake and make amends some day; then he could have them back in front of the audience. He continued to make sure they were well-fed every day and looked-after. He resented having to keep them in a cage, but there was no other choice. It was either this or he would have to hand them over to the authorities. And who knew how they would be treated there. So, he would visit them every night before going to bed to say some kind words to them and hoped in his heart that they would respond to that kindness with more kindness. But that had not happened yet.

Kaalia continued his low-pitched menacing growl, 'That fool of a monkey and that even bigger fool of an elephant think that they are the stars of the show now...I used to be the star attraction before Gulshan barred me from performing and locked us up here! Once I get out, I'll show them who the real boss is!'

Later that night, Mr Gulshan stepped out of his office to start his nightly rounds before he went to bed. His last stop was the cage with the panthers. He peered through its bars to see the panthers lying at the far back, in the shadows.

Sensing someone there, Kaalia opened his eyes to see Mr Gulshan looking at them. He walked up slowly to him, who had a welcoming smile on his face. On seeing Kaalia, Mr Gulshan gently put his hand in between the bars in an attempt to affectionately pet him but Kaalia roared and tried to bite his hand off. With a start he jumped back and stumbled on the ground. Hearing the noise, one of his assistants rushed out of the office and helped him up. Mr Gulshan looked back in the hope that maybe Kaalia would be feeling bad about attacking him, but Kaalia stared back defiantly.

The assistant, in an attempt to make Mr Gulshan feel better, said, 'Sir, some animals remain wild forever, even if you treat them with love.'

A distraught Mr Gulshan looked down and sighed, 'There is good in everyone...we just have to help them find it.'

Chapter 4

The early morning mist was sent scuttling away with the welcome arrival of the rays of the winter sun. It was a busy morning at the circus. All the animals were rehearsing their acts with their trainers. All except Chunky of course, who was walking around with his characteristic carefree swagger, chomping on a banana, when he heard the sound of some classical singing from the nearby tiger enclosure. He stopped to have a closer look. Sitting half-submerged in a cool pond was Pintu Da, the Royal Bengal tiger, rehearsing his classical singing. A crazy idea formed in Chunky's mind and it was too good to resist! He sashayed in.

'Fantastic! You sing so well, Pintu Da! Flowers bloom every time you open your mouth to sing!' Said Chunky, trying to keep as straight a face as he could manage. Pintu Da, always a sucker for praise, beamed with pride.

'Thank you, Chonky Dada! You're the only one around who recognizes true talent. All the others

here are tone-deaf!'

Chunky squatted down, 'You're right! It is only I who appreciates your genius! Your voice has that supreme quality of chalk screeching on a blackboard!'

Having no idea what that was and thinking it was more praise, Pintu Da sang even louder. Chunky continued, 'What a voice! But Dada, the others...especially that fellow...no, let it be...you'll only get upset if I told you...'

His curiosity piqued, Pintu Da stopped singing. 'What? Please tell me? I want to know!'

Chunky tried to keep his face as serious as he possibly could. 'If you insist, Pintu Da. You know that silly Chintu keeps making fun of your singing all the time...'

Pintu Da let out a few sad notes on hearing this. Encouraged, Chunky went on, 'Just a few minutes ago he was saying that...he was saying that...no, let it be...'

'What was he saying? Please tell me!'

'He was saying that if he heard you singing one more time he would come here and beat you up!'

There was silence for a moment, and then

Pintu Da burst out laughing.

'Hahahahaha! That coward? Beat me up? Hahahaha!'

'Pintu Da, these animals that can't appreciate your genius must be taught a lesson. I suggest you sing his name out as loud as you can, just to get back at him!'

'I will do just that. I am going to burst his eardrums with my loud singing!'

Chunky muttered to himself, 'Just like you burst our eardrums everyday with that cacophony of yours!'

'Eh?'

'Oh nothing, nothing, Pintu Da...I have to leave now; you should catch your breath and start singing his name out loud after five minutes!'

Happy with his set-up, Chunky quickly scampered out.

At the lion enclosure, Chintamani was sprawled on a bed of straw rubbing his backside and moaning in pain. Chunky sauntered in and squatted besides Chintamani, who was so caught up with his own troubles that he failed to notice Chunky.

'What's up Chintu?'

Chintamani jumped with a start, and screamed, 'Aaaaahhh!'

He turned to notice Chunky and cried out in his high-pitched voice, 'Oh it's you! You really s... startled me there. And my name is Chintamani, not Chintu!'

'Okay, sorry Chintu!'

'There you go again! As it is I'm in so much pain since yesterday...'

Chunky saw his chance. 'Tch tch...the evil that lurks around here...very sad...why does he trouble you so?'

A curious Chintamani turned to Chunky, 'Who's the one troubling me?'

'No...now let it be...'

'Please! Tell me...who is it that is troubling me?'

Chunky sighed, 'What can I say Chints... The same person who...er...shot you on your...umm... backside yesterday...'

Chintamani sat up straight, 'Who was that? Please, you have to tell me!'

Chunky shrugged knowingly but didn't say anything. Bang on cue, Pintu Da's loud voice came wafting through from across the tiger enclosure.

'OH MY CHINTUUUUUU...'

A cringing Chintamani covered his ears with his paws. So, it must have been that Pintu, he thought. He looked enquiringly at Chunky, who confirmed with a nod and pointed to a garbage bin that was close by, 'Don't be afraid...I'm with you.'

Chintamani got the hint.

At the tiger enclosure Pintu Da was belting out his song as loud as he possibly could, his eyes closed in deep concentration, for he never took his singing lightly even if it was just to rile someone.

'Oooo chintuuuuaaaaaaaa...about music you have no clue...you're a tone-deaf foo-oo-ool, what can we dooooooo...'

His loud singing was interrupted by:

SPLAT!

SPLAT!!

SPLAT!!!

The order in which the contents of the garbage bin landed with a SPLAT! on Pintu Da's face were as follows:

1. Rotten Tomatoes
2. Egg Shells
3. Banana Peels

At the entrance, Chunky, who had just thrown all that at Pintu Da, quickly pushed Chintamani to the front and hid behind him. Pintu Da looked up through the gap in the banana peel that was covering his eyes. He saw Chintamani there, only a few feet away from him. His blood started to boil.

'I'm right behind you, Chints! Be brave!' Chunky whispered.

Chintamani was nervous about the impending confrontation but since he had support, he tried to put up a brave front. Pintu Da rushed forward and confronted him with a roar so loud that it gave Chintamani goosebumps!

'Firstly, you make fun of my singing and secondly, you throw garbage at me!'

Chunky nudged Chintamani from behind,

who then mustered up a wee bit of courage and responded in his shrill voice, 'You k-keep troubling me all the time!'

He then turned to look behind him to get some support, but Chunky wasn't there anymore! When he looked in the front again, Pintu Da was glowering at him. Whatever semblance of courage was left in him withered away. 'S-s-s-s-see...P-P-Pintu...th-th-this will not d-d-d-do!'

Pintu Da began circling round Chintamani. 'You puny lion! You dare throw garbage at me!'

'Uh-h-h...then wh-why do you t-t-t-trouble me so...?'

Pintu Da growled some more, 'Trouble? I'll give you trouble!'

He pounced on Chintamani and they both started rolling on the ground. They then got up and started scuffling. Well, to be more accurate Pintu scuffled and Chintu blocked.

Hidden away behind the tree by the entrance of the enclosure, Chunky burst out laughing. His prank had worked! He loved it! He started laughing so hard that he was soon rolling on the floor. As he turned he saw Bhole Ram, with

Uncle Geri perched on his ear, walking towards the enclosure to see what the commotion was about. He quickly got up and looked around for a place to hide himself from where he could have a vantage point to watch what happened next. The tree by which he was standing would do the job perfectly, so he quickly scurried up.

On seeing these two big cats engaged in a mighty scuffle, Bhole Ram hurried to break the fight. With one swoop of his trunk he separated the two. 'What is wrong with the two of you? Why are you fighting like children?'

Pintu Da, almost breathing fumes out of his nose, pointed to Chintamani. 'He...he threw garbage on my face! He keeps saying that I sing terribly and burst everyone's eardrums with my singing!'

Although nervous, Chintamani had to defend himself. And that he did, but with a wail. 'Uh... that's b-because he shot at me with a fat, round stone yesterday...on my b-backside!'

'I did not!' interjected Pintu Da.

Sensing something, Bhole Ram shushed both of them up and tried to clear things up. He turned to Chintamani first. 'Who told you that Pintu Da shot you on your...er...backside?'

'Chunky did! He's my friend after all!' He justified.

Next, Bhole Ram turned to Pintu Da, 'And who told you that Chintamani ridicules your singing abilities?'

Pintu Da was about to reply when Bhole Ram interrupted him, 'Wait, let me guess. It was Chunky...right?'

Pintu Da nodded in the affirmative, 'He's my friend after all!'

Uncle Geri, who was watching the proceedings silently up until now, flew into the fray. 'This is a classic set-up! While you both are fighting like little children, Chunky, the one responsible for this entire mess is hiding in that tree and enjoying himself to the hilt!'

In one synchronized motion, all the parties involved in this incident turned to the said tree. As if on cue, the leaves on some of the top branches started shaking with mirth. Bhole Ram stepped forward and shook it with his strong trunk and like a ripe mango Chunky fell from the top branches on to the ground.

If Bhole Ram had hands, he would have placed them on his hips. But since he didn't, he just stared down at Chunky waiting for an explanation. Chunky got up calmly and noticed everyone staring down at him. He coolly brushed the dust off himself and looked up at everyone, 'Chints...Pints...' Then he suddenly shouted out: 'GOT YOU!' He burst out laughing and darted off. All were left staring into empty space.

Bhole Ram sighed, 'How do you solve a problem like Chunky?'

Chapter 5

'I'm sure he must be hiding somewhere in these bushes.'

Pintu Da, followed by Bhole Ram and Uncle Geri, with Chintamani several steps behind them, comprised the search party that was looking for Chunky. Moments after he had dashed off, they decided it would be in everybody's best interests to track him down and give him a collective piece of their mind. His pranks were getting out of control. They had spent the better part of the last few hours searching for him. The cold breeze had picked up and the sky was slowly getting overcast. They would soon have to abandon the search.

Pintu Da was right. Chunky was indeed hiding in the bushes that they were all standing next to. There was no way Chunky could get out of there without them noticing. Just as he started scratching his head to come up with a solution, a pair of hands grabbed him by the scruff of his neck and before he knew it, he was whisked all the way up to the branch of a nearby high tree. Chunky turned round to see the pretty girl monkey Jenny, his best friend in the whole wide world, in front of him.

'Jenny! You rescued me once again! What would I ever do without you? Wasn't that fun?'

Jenny had a lissome frame, dancing dark eyes and as far as girl monkeys go, she was as pretty as they come. But all this was lost on Chunky who somehow never noticed her beauty and sweet nature. His attention was always on the pranks. She leaned forward and put a finger on his lips. 'Shhhh! We'll talk about your prank later. For now, I suggest you go off to the secret hiding place behind those rocks and wait there till everything cools down.'

Chunky beamed happily and gave Jenny a friendly slap on the back. He whispered to her, 'Jenny dear, you're an absolute darling...and my best friend in the whole world!'

He leaned forward and gave her an affectionate peck on her cheek. As usual, her eyes lit up with a twinkle, and her cheeks blushed a rosy pink. Chunky jumped up on to the higher branch and waved at her, 'See you later, Jenny!' and he was off.

Jenny sighed as she watched him swing away. She touched her cheek longingly where he had given her a peck. She clearly had LOVE written in bold in her eyes!

Later that night, it had gotten more windy. Bhole Ram, with Uncle Geri hovering under his big ear had huddled into a corner of the elephant enclosure. He was visibly upset with the events of the day and was venting his feelings out.

'That Chunky! He's always causing trouble. Doesn't he realize how lucky we are to be a part of Mr Gulshan's circus?'

Uncle Geri nodded. He totally agreed with Bhole Ram. Other circus-owners didn't treat their animals with half the respect, love and care that they were treated with here at The Great Indian Circus. They were allowed to roam free as they pleased and mingle with one another on the huge circus grounds when not rehearsing. In other circuses, animals were always kept in cages and let out only during performances. Here Mr Gulshan made sure they were fed well and looked after all the time. His staff was always so loving and attentive towards the animals. It was a model circus. Bhole Ram was worried that if Chunky continued with his pranks, Mr Gulshan might get annoyed and start treating all the animals like the other circus-owners do.

A shuffling sound broke the thoughtful silence. Bhole Ram and Uncle Geri looked up to notice Savitri standing a short distance away. As it always happened at the arrival of Savitri, Bhole Ram's heart skipped a beat. The two elephants stood there in awkward silence fluttering their respective eyelashes at each other but not uttering a word. Seeing this, Uncle Geri shook his head. These two were useless. This love story wouldn't move forward unless one of them made a move. Uncle Geri decided to take matters into his own wings and flew behind Bhole Ram's ear where he could stay hidden but yet be able to pass on instructions to Bhole Ram. From this vantage point, he whispered loud enough for Bhole Ram to be able to listen.

'Go on! Don't just stand there! Open your big fat mouth and ask her in!'

Taking the cue, a few words somehow bravely found their way out of Bhole Ram's mouth, 'Uh...H...hi, Savitri...umm...why don't you come in...?'

Savitri walked in shyly. Thank you. Uh...I heard about the commotion earlier today...that Chintamani and Pintu Da had some sort of fight...I also heard that you sorted out the problem...so...I just wanted to come and see how you were doing. You must have had a long day...'

Bhole Ram couldn't believe his lucky ears! Uncle Geri goaded him on from behind his right ear, 'Go on! Tell her you love her...what are you waiting for? You know she likes you too, otherwise why would she come here?'

Savitri looked on curiously and wondered why Bhole Ram was nodding his head and muttering to himself.

'Go on you big baby! Tell her...NOW!' Uncle Geri went on.

'NO WAY!' objected Bhole Ram loudly.

'Uh...excuse me?' Savitri was a little taken aback.

'Uh...no! I'm s...sorry, I didn't mean that...uh...please...do come in...'

She slowly started to walk closer to him. Uncle Geri was happy and goaded Bhole Ram some more, 'Now don't waste time...just tell her how you feel!'

Bhole Ram was feeling the pressure and wanted to be alone with Savitri. He turned his head slightly towards Uncle Geri and snapped, 'Fine! Just go now...please!'

Savitri stopped in her tracks. These were clearly mixed signals Bhole Ram was sending out. She didn't know what to make of it.

Seeing her stop in her tracks, Bhole Ram stuttered, 'Uh...n-not you! P...please...come in...'

Savitri took a moment to get her thoughts together, since Bhole Ram was behaving peculiarly. She took a hesitant step towards him.

Uncle Geri, satisfied with the situation, decided to leave the two lovebirds alone.

'Good luck, Romeo!' And he flew off.

'Okay...goodbye!' Said Bhole Ram before he saw Savitri raising her eyebrows. 'Uh...sorry...I meant good evening.'

Bhole Ram was behaving stranger than

usual. Nevertheless, she walked in. They smiled awkwardly at each other. Bhole Ram cleared his throat, 'Ahem...Savitri...if I may say so...you've put on some weight...you're looking even bigger and pleasantly plumper now than you were some days ago.'

Savitri blushed. That was the sweetest thing any elephant had ever said to her. And it was the first time Bhole Ram had paid her such a wonderful compliment.

Encouraged by her blushing cheeks, Bhole Ram shuffled his feet and looked shyly at the grass below before continuing, 'Uh...I've been wanting to tell you this for a while now...you see the thing is...I...I...l...'

'AAAAAAAAHHHHHHHHHH!' Savitri screamed out loud.

Bhole Ram looked up to see a spider dangling in front of Savitri's eyes. She looked absolutely terrified and before Bhole Ram could do anything about it, she turned around and dashed off to her corner at the far end of the enclosure. His possible moment of glory was splintered into countless pieces.

There was some sort of muted guffawing sound that Bhole Ram heard from somewhere up in the trees. He jerked his head up to see Chunky on one of the branches, covering his mouth with one hand and shaking with laughter. In his other hand was a spider web at the end of which the aforementioned spider was dangling. Bhole Ram gave Chunky a dirty look, but decided to go after Savitri and see how she was doing.

'You should be ashamed of yourself, Chunky!'

Chunky turned around with a start to see Jenny standing right behind him on the branches. He smiled, for he was always happy to see her, even though she didn't share the same love for pranks as he did and lectured him every time she caught him playing one.

'Why are you always up to mischief? Troubling friends like this is not good...isn't it time you got a bit serious in life?'

Chunky threw his arms up in the air, 'Here you go preaching again!'

Jenny sat him down and reminded him of how Bhole Ram looked after all the animals and they all looked up to him. There was a fire in the circus some time ago and it was Bhole Ram who rescued all the animals and then helped Mr Gulshan and the staff in putting out the fire. He had saved the circus and all their lives that day.

Chunky leaned back against the bark of the tree. 'I was just having a little fun! No one seems to have a sense of humour around here anymore!'

Jenny was serious this time, 'I think you should go to both of them and say sorry. Make amends for what you did...right now!'

Chunky tried protesting but Jenny shushed him up. 'No excuses! Don't I rescue you and hide you every time you play your stupid pranks? Can't you do this much for me?'

Chunky knew better than to argue with Jenny when she was in such a mood. He jumped on to the branches and started to swing away, muttering to himself, 'Hmph! A genius is never appreciated in his time!'

Jenny looked at him as he swung away and thought to herself, 'If only you knew what I feel for you...I wish you stopped playing these silly pranks and got a bit serious in life.'

The leaves on the ground flew as the breeze became stronger. The moon was almost obscured by clouds. Bhole Ram looked to the other side of the elephant enclosure where he saw Savitri still trembling with fear. He walked up to her side and almost touched her trunk with his in order to comfort her when his shyness got the better of him. 'Uh...Savitri...don't worry about the spiders too much...we all have our fears.'

Comforted by his presence, she looked into his eyes and smiled. They continued looking into each other's eyes for a few moments when a few rolls of thunder followed with some flashes of lightning. It had started to drizzle. Bhole Ram looked up at the sky. He gestured to Savitri that they should go take shelter under the stand of oak trees, where they would find protection from the rain.

Once there, Bhole Ram plucked out some big branches with his trunk and used them to shield Savitri from the rain. She looked into his eyes and gave him a gentle smile. Chunky, who was swinging by on the branches above those very oak trees, saw the two elephants.

'Hmmm, what do we have here now? A cozy little moment, eh.' He thought to himself.

Down below, Savitri spoke shyly, 'That's so sweet of you Bhole Ram...'

'Uh...Savitri...you could call me Bhole...just Bhole...'

If it wasn't a rainy night and if the sun had been out, you would have noticed both the elephants blush a shade of pink. Anyway, Chunky had stopped moving on the branches above to eavesdrop on their conversation. 'Dude! These two are so mushy! I'm gonna be sick!' He muttered to himself.

Bhole Ram cleared his throat and mustered the courage for the second time that evening. 'Um... Savitri...there's something I've been wanting to tell you for a while now...you see...er...'

This was too good to resist for Chunky. In the battle between his do-gooder side and mischievous side, the latter always won. He changed his voice to pretend like someone was having a conversation with him and spoke loud enough for the two elephants below to hear.

'Hey, Chunky! That Bhole Ram is too funny, eh!

So, he actually paid you to dangle that spider in front of Savitri?'

Both the elephants looked up, but as the leaves above were very dense and the rain was coming down they couldn't really see much.

Chunky continued his one-man act, changing back to his own voice. 'Hahaha! Yeah! And guess what? This time he told me to dangle an even bigger spider in front of her to frighten her some more!'

Savitri looked back sharply at Bhole Ram, aghast at what she was overhearing. Bhole Ram panicked and all the courage he had mustered went diving back into the depths from which it had emerged.

'S...Savitri...please...it's that Chunky again...up to no good...he's just...'

'Telling the truth?' Interrupted Savitri.

Bhole Ram struggled to proclaim his innocence.

'No...no...believe me...he's a prankster...'

A tear started to well up in Savitri's right eye. As if matching the mood, the cold rain from the skies started to come down heavier.

Chunky was really enjoying himself. He continued the charade in his own voice. 'Bhole Ram told me Savitri would never suspect him of playing such a prank on her. She assumes he's such an innocent, sweet guy! He's totally taking advantage of that...hahaha!'

Not to be left behind, her left eye too started to form a big fat tear. 'I really liked you...I thought you were different...I guess I was wrong...'

She stepped back as Bhole Ram tried his best to reason with her. 'Please believe me, Savitri. I would never do that to anyone, least of all you!'

With grief in her eyes Savitri turned to leave. Bhole Ram tried protesting but it fell on deaf ears as Savitri walked away in the rain.

Bhole Ram stood there rooted to the spot, too stunned to speak anymore. He heard a familiar chuckle from above. That Chunky again! He looked up to see Chunky rolling over with laughter. Bhole Ram's turned red with rage. 'Chunky! I'm going to get back at you for this!'

He wrapped his mighty trunk around the tree and gave it a good shake. Chunky dropped out of the tree like a ripened fruit and started laughing out louder as he brushed off the wet mud from his fur. 'Catch me if you can!' He winked at Bhole Ram and dashed off. After a moment's hesitation, Bhole Ram decided this time he wouldn't let Chunky get away with his prank. He chased him.

There was a gale blowing and lightning streaked menacingly across the cold, wet night sky.

Chapter 6

The icy rain was pelting down hard. Chunky was laughing uncontrollably while running. He paused for breath and turned around to see Bhole Ram some distance away, waddling through the puddles trying to catch up with him. Chunky splashed off through the puddles again, taking a sudden left towards the big circus tent. Once he got there, he skidded under the canvas and in the next second he was inside. He thought he'd definitely be safe inside. There was a loud cracking sound as the thunder rumbled outside.

Bhole Ram, however, had seen Chunky dive under the canvas, so he wobbled away as fast as he could towards the main entrance to enter from there. There was no way he would be able to dive under the canvas like Chunky had. Once inside, it took him a few seconds to adjust to the darkness.

Bhole Ram heard a snicker from somewhere ahead. He turned to see Chunky scurrying up the rope ladder leading to the trapeze platform. In a flash, he had climbed up. He looked down at Bhole Ram and shouted out a challenge, his voice echoing in the vast empty space, 'Yoohoo big boy! Up here! Why don't you come up and get me!'

Bhole Ram narrowed his eyes as a look of determination spread across his face. With focused steps he walked to the base of the ladder and looked up. Chunky was smirking. There was no way on earth that this big bumbling elephant could ever climb up and get to him now. But determination sometimes makes us do the most unexpected things. Bhole Ram heaved his weight up on to the ladder, slowly and steadily pulling his mass up with the help of his powerful trunk and making his way up the ladder, step by step, precariously. Chunky was shocked at first, but then as always he saw its funny side and started to chuckle. A big, mighty elephant huffing and puffing his way up a flimsy rope ladder was not a sight one got to witness every day! He was bringing out talents in Bhole Ram he never knew existed!

'Ladies and gentlemen, boys and girls! Presenting now a miracle—the climbing elephant!'

Bhole Ram, of course, didn't find anything remotely funny about the whole exercise. He was almost at the top now and with one big monumental lurch, he found himself up on the trapeze platform. If he hadn't been so angry, he would have been real proud of this unimaginable feat! But he was very angry and this was not a time for self-congratulating. He had a mission. He took a moment to catch his breath and then realized that Chunky was nowhere on the trapeze platform. No sooner had Bhole Ram performed the near impossible feat of getting all the way up onto the trapeze platform, than Chunky flung himself up onto the trapeze and was now swinging high above the safety net below. He landed on the trapeze platform on other side and waving at Bhole Ram shouted, 'Come and get me!'

Outside, lightning flashed ferociously across the night sky and was followed by a deafening clap of thunder. The rain was coming down even heavier on the roof of the circus tent, so much so that one could hear it loud and clear inside the tent too.

Seeing Bhole Ram just standing there, Chunky

held on tight to the trapeze and swung himself towards the other side, as if to tease him, 'What are you waiting for? Catch me!'

Just as Chunky was about to start laughing again, he stopped himself. Ahead, a determined Bhole Ram had heaved himself with the help of his trunk onto the trapeze and with a push of his hind leg he had started swinging the trapeze towards Chunky while precariously balancing his girth on it. The frame holding up the trapezes groaned under the weight.

Both the trapezes swung by each other as lightning flashed outside. Reaching the end of their arc, the two swung by again and this time Bhole Ram stretched his trunk outwards in an attempt to catch Chunky. He missed. The trapezes swung by once again and just then at that very moment outside, a blaze of lightning struck the metal pole above the big circus tent and a sizzling current of electricity shot down the pole on to the steel beams holding the trapezes. Bhole Ram once again stretched out his trunk and this time he did make contact with Chunky.

The current of lightning zapped down to

the two swinging trapezes and hit both Bhole Ram and Chunky just as they made contact. CRAAACK!

The electric voltage sizzled through their bodies stunning them completely out of their wits. With that colossal impact, they lost their grips on the trapezes, flung backwards and then came crashing down towards the safety net. The net however was no match for Bhole Ram's bulk, and the two ripped through the net and fell hard onto the ground at a distance from one another, stunned unconscious!

The night fell silent. For a few moments it seemed like the world had stopped turning. The monkey and the elephant lay there, passed out. And then, an extraordinary thing happened. From their bodies arose two big spheres of blinding white light that floated up in the air above them. They shimmered there for a few moments, lighting everything around them in a dazzling golden glow. It was as if the spheres were unsure whether to soar into the heavens or go back to the bodies of the animals they had just exited. This uncertainty made the spheres tremble and they started spinning around one another. They spun. And spun. And spun. And then abruptly, the orb of light that had emerged from Bhole Ram's body descended into Chunky's and the one from Chunky's body descended into Bhole Ram's.

By some sort of heavenly error, their souls had switched bodies...it was a cosmic cross connection! The universe was surely upto some monkey business!

Chapter 7

The cacophony of a hundred birds chirping loudly and the feeling of a sledgehammer pounding away in some corner of his head was the first thing Chunky remembered on regaining consciousness. Slowly, the loud noise of the birds faded away and what remained was only the dull throbbing in his head. He gingerly opened his eyes and adjusted them to the brightness of the morning only to see the faces of Savitri, Chintamani, Pintu Da and Uncle Geri staring down at him with a look of concern.

'AAAAAHHHHH! Uh...don't hit me, please! My head hurts!' Screamed Chunky, as he recalled the prank he played the night before. Obviously, these animals had come to catch him and teach him a lesson, right?

Wrong! Instead of grabbing him, they were looking at him with utmost concern as he lay there on the ground. Still, he was sure they would pounce on him any moment.

'Look...I meant no harm...it was a silly prank... okay...I won't play pranks anymore...promise! Just let me go.' He explained with a nervous quiver in his voice.

Pintu Da extended his powerful paw towards Chunky's head. 'Let me touch you and see if you're fine.'

'AAAAAHHHHH! Please! Don't hurt me!' screamed out Chunky as he tried standing up to run away before these animals started to beat him up.

As he stood up to run, he realized that he actually stood up to a great height, a lot higher than ground level, and could see much more than what he was accustomed to seeing when he stood up. Chunky panicked and started to run helter-skelter, barely managing to balance himself. He couldn't understand what was happening. He bobbed and swayed his way out of the tent as fast as he could.

In this state of bewilderment, Chunky continued running past the animal enclosures that were behind the main circus tent, broke through the makeshift gate and towards the little stream that flowed behind the circus, his sight bobbing as he looked down from this unaccustomed height. He splashed into the stream and finally stopped. He stood there panting, dazed and confused while he muttered to himself,

'What just happened there? Why was I feeling so strange while running?'

His gaze shifted downwards as he bent down to sip some water. His reflection came into view...and instead of seeing his own reflection; he saw Bhole Ram's reflection staring back at him instead!

'AAAAAAHHHHHHH! NOOOOOOOO!' He screamed out.

The other animals were running towards him. A concerned Uncle Geri flew up close to him, 'Are you feeling alright, Bhole Ram?'

Chintamani took a tentative step towards him too, 'Uh...Bhole Ram, there was a raging storm last night and we were all huddled in our enclosures so we don't know what happened. When we woke up and went to the tent...we saw you sprawled on the ground, unconscious.'

A puzzled Chunky turned to look at the animals. Why were they behaving so strange? And more importantly, why on earth were they calling him Bhole Ram? He turned once more to look at his reflection in the water. Bhole Ram's reflection stared back at him once again.

'NOOOOOOOOO!' He cried out. He tried to put his hands up to touch his face but all he could see was a big fat elephant trunk coming towards his eyes.

'AAAAAAHHHHHHH!'

He couldn't fathom what was happening to him.

Uncle Geri once again flapped his little wings and came up to Chunky, 'What has happened Bhole Ram? It seems you had a fall from the trapeze platform...the safety net was ripped apart. How did you manage to climb up there in the first place?'

All the others present echoed Uncle Geri's concerns, 'Please tell us Bhole Ram!'

Looking left and then right, Chunky looked at all of them. He had never been so stumped ever before. What was going on?

His voice started trembling with fear as he started to speak, 'L...l...look, why are all of you calling me B…Bhole Ram? I have no clue what's g-going on…p…p…please…I'm very sorry…I will never play pranks again…please leave me alone for a l…little while. I don't know what's h…happening to me…'

Uncle Geri thought it best that Bhole Ram get some rest. 'Okay, everybody…let's leave him alone for a little while…he's hurt his head real bad.'

The animals started to walk away. Chintamani shook his head and spoke in his shrill voice, 'He had a great fall, just like Humpty-Dumpty did.'

Bhole Ram slowly opened his eyes. It was aching all over. He could see the roof of the tent far above him. The memory of the previous night's events was there in his head but all scrambled up at the moment. He tried standing up but for some reason felt very strange doing so. When he finally stood up, he realized he wasn't very far up from the ground as he usually was when standing. He brought his trunk up towards his face, but instead of seeing his trunk he saw a pair of tiny monkey hands coming towards his face. He froze.

Where was his trunk? And why did he see a pair of tiny monkey hands? The sound of some voices approaching from the tent entrance took his attention away for a moment.

The group that had stepped out was walking back into the tent. Uncle Geri was leading the pack, talking to all of them, 'Yes, let Bhole Ram rest outside for a bit. We should check that safety net and figure out how he fell.' He looked back and saw the monkey standing there a short distance ahead, looking dazed. 'There he is, all awake now. He is always causing trouble. This time it seems even worse than usual.'

All of them rushed towards him. Bhole Ram was quite relieved to see all his friends there. He needed their help to understand why he was feeling so strange. He smiled in relief as they came closer but for some reason they were not smiling back and were instead scowling at him. As they got close, they pounced on him and started roughing him up! Pintu Da shook him up a little and sang out loud, 'Oooohhhhhh Chonky...What did you do to poo...oor Bhole Ram? You made him fall...fall...fall all the way up from there?'

A baffled Bhole Ram struggled to get away from their clutches and let out a barrage of questions, 'OW! STOP! Please... Why are you all pushing me around? And what are you talking about? Why are you calling me Chunky? Why would I drop myself...and from where?'

They all started to rough him up again. Uncle Geri started flying in a circle around Bhole Ram, which made the latter's head spin even more. 'Don't try and be over-smart now! How did Bhole Ram get hurt? I'm sure you had something to do with it!'

Poor Bhole Ram—he had no clue what was going on! 'My head is aching right now so please stop pushing me around like this! And one moment...why are you talking to me like I'm not here?'

The gang started being violent with him once again. Bhole Ram, now starting to really panic, protested as earnestly as he could—'Please...I'm your friend...why are you doing this...something is wrong here...and where is my trunk?'

They all pounced on him in one big huddle. Bhole Ram struggled under all that weight, but then he saw an opening between Chintamani's legs. He squeezed himself towards the gap and after a brief struggle, slipped out through it. It surprised him that he could squeeze through so tiny a space. He caught his breath for a moment and then before anyone realized it, dashed off to safety.

Bhole Ram got that strange feeling again while running. He couldn't understand it.

'What on earth is happening? Why am I so close to the ground while running?'

Clumsily, he ran towards the little stream and splashed into it, hoping the cold water would clear up this entire muddle. He was very tired and needed some cold water to drink. As he bent down to douse his trunk in the refreshing stream, the reflection that stared back at him scared him out of his wits. Instead of seeing his own face reflected back at him, he could only see Chunky's!

'AAAAAAAAAAHHHHHHHH!' He screamed.

From a little distance away, as if echoing his own scream, Bhole Ram heard another scream. Startled, he looked up towards the direction of the sound. The sight that greeted him shook him to

the very bone. A few metres away he saw himself, in the flesh, staring down at him!

Chunky who had looked up when he heard the scream too, was frozen with fear. For the image he saw only a few metres away was of none other than himself!

'AAAAAAAAAAAAAAAAHHHHHHHHHHHHHHHH!' He shrieked too in utter disbelief, confusion, bewilderment, bafflement, perplexity... well, I could go on, but you get the drift.

Seeing him scream, Bhole Ram on the other end screamed again, this time a bit more loudly.

'AAAAAAAAAAAAAAAAHHHHHHHHHHHHHHH!'

For reasons unknown to them, Bhole Ram was now in Chunky's body, and Chunky in Bhole Ram's. Such confusion!

Chapter 8

The silence was deafening. It was as if the earth stood still. The monkey and the elephant stared at each other for several moments in absolute disbelief. Slowly, they started to take tentative steps towards each other, both their minds racing to figure out what was happening. On coming close, Chunky, who was now in Bhole Ram's massive body, and Bhole Ram, who was now in Chunky's small, wiry body, stopped and gaped at each other a little more. To the casual passer-by this scene wouldn't have warranted a second look. It was after all a monkey and an elephant by a stream looking at each other, probably conversing in some animal language. But little would that passer-by know what was actually going on.

Bhole Ram reached out with what he was hoping to be his trunk but was actually a small monkey hand, and Chunky stooped down and reached out with what he thought would be a tiny monkey hand but was actually an elephant's trunk, to touch each other's faces. After a few moments, they turned to look into the water at their reflections. They then looked back at each other, astonished.

Chunky was the first to find his voice, 'Dude! I'm standing in front of me...but when I look through the water, in the reflection I see Bhole staring at me!'

Bhole Ram agreed, 'And I am reaching out to you but it seems I am touching my own face, right in front of me... Oh my God! What is going on...?'

Chunky heaved his massive elephant body back a step. 'You know...I think it's the fall we had... and the electric shock we got from the lightning...I think that explains it all.'

Bhole Ram, intrigued at this possibility, moved his tiny monkey body a step back too.

'You mean that accident...it has made me into you...?'

Chunky nodded in the affirmative, 'And me into you. So bizarre!'

Bhole Ram's heart started pounding. He stuttered out, 'Oh my God! This cannot be happening!'

Convinced this had to be the reason, Chunky looked down at his tummy—'Oh man...am I fat!'

Pintu Da, Chintamani, Savitri and Uncle Geri hurried towards the two confused animals. Uncle Geri had spotted them by the stream.

'There they are! That Chunky must be up to another one of his pranks!'

Uncle Geri turned to the two big cats to order them, 'Pintu and Chintamani, go catch that trouble-making monkey. Make sure he doesn't get away!' He then flew off towards Chunky, now an elephant, thinking him to be Bhole Ram. Savitri, obviously very concerned about her Bhole Ram, stepped closer to the elephant.

Chunky, seeing Uncle Geri flying towards him and Savitri stepping closer, tried to run off. Uncle Geri couldn't understand why the elephant was running away. He flapped his wings harder and caught up with him. 'Oye, Bhole Ram! Why are you running away from me? Stop!'

On hearing this, Chunky stopped. He looked into the stream and remembered that he was now in Bhole Ram's body.

At a short distance away, Bhole Ram who

was now in Chunky's body, noticed Pintu Da and Chintamani charging towards him. Pintu Da didn't seem to have a very friendly expression on his face as he sang out, 'You stoo-oopid monkey Chonky! You will not...will not...will not escape us this time!'

Bhole Ram turned to look into the water and saw Chunky's reflection staring back at him. These two big cats were charging at him because they thought him to be Chunky. He had to explain!

'Wait! There seems to be a mix-up! I can explain every...' Before he could complete his sentence, Pintu Da and Chintamani ambushed him. Bhole Ram tried to wiggle out from under their clutches trying to explain that he wasn't Chunky the monkey, but there was no way his argument was going to be convincing enough! Pintu Da gagged Bhole Ram's mouth with his paw. Seeing that the monkey was cornered, Uncle Geri flew up to them. 'We must teach this troublemaker Chunky a lesson he will never forget!'

Bhole Ram shook his head violently trying to protest, but he was no match for the physical strength of Pintu Da.

Uncle Geri turned to the lion, 'Chintamani, throw him in the small cage, the one next to Kaalia's.'

Chintamani got a little nervous on being given that task. He shook his head at Uncle Geri, 'Uh! Me! Go next to K...Kaalia's cage? No! P...p...lease don't make me do that. He's a scary panther!'

Uncle Geri shook his head, 'You and your anxieties! Fine. Pintu Da will throw him in the cage next to Kaalia's.'

Pintu Da happily broke into a little song 'Haaaa-aaa-aaaa-aaaaaaa...of course... with pleasure!'

On hearing that order from Uncle Geri, Chunky heaved a sigh of relief. In spite of all that had happened, at least it wasn't him being locked up near Kaalia. He was indeed happy to be in Bhole Ram's body, where he was momentarily secure. He thought to himself, 'Hmm! Being a big elephant isn't such a bad thing. Imagine, it could have been me being thrown into the cage close to those ferocious panthers. This has turned out to be quite a stroke of good luck after all!'

Uncle Geri looked at Chunky with sympathy,

'Bhole Ram, son, you go to the enclosure and have a good rest. I'll have someone get you some food.'

This was getting even more interesting for Chunky. He smiled innocently at Uncle Geri and then turned to Bhole Ram and gave him a naughty wink. Enraged, Bhole Ram broke free momentarily from the clutches of Pintu Da and screamed, trying his best to proclaim his innocence, 'Please try and understand! I am Bhole Ram! Somehow, I am in Chunky's body! Please! Somebody please believe me!'

On hearing this seemingly ludicrous story, Pintu Da gagged him again. Uncle Geri turned to Pintu Da, 'Quickly lock him up before he tries another trick and runs off.'

Pintu Da dragged a struggling Bhole Ram towards the cage. Chunky looked at the struggling Bhole and smiled roguishly as Uncle Geri escorted him to the elephant enclosure.

Savitri heaved a sigh of relief thinking poor Bhole Ram would finally get some rest. Little did she know what the truth was.

Chapter 9

It was even colder in the area where the cages were. Clasped tightly by the scruff of his neck between the powerful jaws of Pintu Da, Bhole Ram was carried there and then dropped with a thud onto the muddy ground. Dusting himself off, Bhole Ram looked up to see the big cage where Kaalia and his cronies were locked up. At the far end of the cage was another section separated from the main cage by a thin grill. That was where he would soon be locked too. He felt chilled to his bones.

Pintu Da opened the side door and lifted a struggling Bhole Ram up again, who tried pleading, 'Please! Don't lock me in there…I'm your friend Bhole…' Before he could complete his sentence, he was flung in and locked up. Pintu Da and Chintamani smiled proudly at the completion of their task and the knowledge that Chunky the prankster was about to get the lesson of his life!

From the cold shadows at the far end of the cage rumbled a low-pitched, ominous growl. The colour drained from Chintamani's face, 'P...Pintu Da...I think we should leave now...' Facing Kaalia was not one of his favourite activities. Or anyone's for that matter. Pintu Da nodded, it was time to head back to the others. Bhole Ram was now all by himself. He swallowed hard as he gazed ahead into the dark shadows of the cage beyond his grill. A shiver ran down his spine.

As far as winter mornings go, the next morning was as cold as they come. To provide some much needed relief, the sun was out and about, shining brightly, trying its best to mix warmth in the winter air. The birds were chirping happily in the trees. 'It is a beautiful day,' thought Chunky to himself. Life was good! Just a few moments earlier, Pintu Da and Chintamani had left him a big bunch of bananas wrapped in its leaves. Yesterday, these two big cats were waiting to get their powerful paws on Chunky, but today they were pampering him! Mr Gulshan had also stopped by and left a big bucket of rice balls for him to eat. The accidental switching of bodies wasn't so bad after all. This was a life Chunky could get used to!

The familiar flap of wings told him he had another visitor.

'What's up, Geri?'

Uncle Geri almost dropped in mid-flight as he heard this greeting. Bhole Ram had never spoken to him this way. Must be that hard knock on his head when he fell, thought Uncle Geri.

'Uh...hope you feel better soon...will come back later...see you!'

'Wouldn't wanna be you!' Shrugged Chunky.

That head injury seemed worse than expected, thought Uncle Geri as he flew off.

As a monkey, one of the naughty things Chunky had learnt was to make fermented fruit and coconut juice. It was an acquired skill, but Chunky had mastered it and every once in a while he used to mix it in the water meant for the animals to drink. Then he'd enjoy the results as the animals who drank that water would get a bit tipsy and sway drunkenly as they walked. Chunky was feeling so different, he thought he'd make some and enjoy a few sips of the juice himself.

And enjoy a few sips he did. More than just a few sips, to be honest. A satisfied beam spread over Chunky's face as he drifted off into a happy dreamland. A short while later, Savitri came to check on him. Seeing him peacefully asleep, she smiled affectionately and gently patted his forehead with her trunk. Chunky woke up with a start and saw her in front of him with her trunk on his head.

'Ewww! What are you doing? I was fast asleep!'

This was not the greeting she expected from Bhole Ram. She was taken aback at first but then she thought of the accident he had. 'Sorry...I didn't mean to disturb you. The thing is, I was really worried when I heard about your accident and that you were unconscious for a while...I just wanted to see if you were doing fine,' she said sweetly.

Chunky rolled his eyes up. He muttered to himself, 'Dude! This is so full of mush! I could puke!'

'Sorry? Did you say something?'

'Er... not at all, please go on,' said Chunky with

a bored expression.

This was so unlike Bhole Ram, she thought to herself. With a look of concern, she continued, 'I was saying that I was so scared when I heard...you know, everyone here looks upto you and I am...oh I mean we all are extremely fond of you.'

Chunky stifled a yawn, waiting for her to end her speech. She went on, shyly looking down at her feet as she spoke, 'If anything were to happen to you I would...I mean we would all not be able to handle it.'

Chunky's uninterested eyes started to wander when he spotted a spider dangling from the tree branches above, while Savitri was pouring her heart out. His eyes lit up. She was speaking softly now, getting a bit more emotional. 'I hope you get completely well soon...for us and for the people who come to see the circus...we all love...I mean like you very much.' She looked up only to see him dangling a frightening hairy spider in front of her eyes with his trunk.

'AAAAAAAHHHHH!' Screamed Savitri and ran towards her side of the enclosure. When she looked at him, he was laughing away merrily.

'I thought you were different!' She shouted.

On hearing this, Chunky guffawed even louder and yelled back, 'Different? Hahaha! Yes, of course! And the spider...that was for your boring speech!'

A tear rolled down Savitri's cheek.

Bhole Ram heaved a temporary sigh of relief. It had been a long while since he had been locked, but as of yet there was no movement from the shadows at the other end. He could hear some distant rumblings and growls but none of the panthers had come up to his side of the cage. He looked out through the cold bars of steel and resumed his thoughts about the astonishing and unbelievable incidents that led to him being here. He was busy pondering when his chain of thought was broken by a friendly voice.

'How are you?'

It was Jenny. She had been awfully concerned and had come to the cage to see how Chunky was doing. She had brought a bunch of bananas for him to eat and shyly gave them to him.

'Hmmm...she has a soft corner for that prankster monkey...how could a good girl like her have feelings for a trouble-maker like him? Poor girl,' thought Bhole Ram. He took the offering from Jenny, awkward as to what to say next. Hungry and tired, he peeled one of the bananas and quietly started chomping on it with a feeling of gratitude.

Jenny felt a surge of compassion and affection on seeing him so hungrily devour the bananas. 'I know now is not the right time to do an "I told you so", but I don't like it when everyone says bad things about you...I don't like it when you're locked up like this.'

Bhole Ram looked up at her and nodded, 'I don't like it either, sister...' and he diverted his attention back to the fruit in front of him.

'Sister?!' Jenny was quite taken aback and disheartened on being addressed so.

Bhole Ram looked up again at her, not understanding.

'Did I say something wrong, sister?'

Jenny couldn't believe his attitude. 'You're kidding around even at a time like this, Chunky?'

A tear dropped from her eye.

Bhole Ram realized why she was feeling bad and tried explaining, 'No...no...please try and understand...I'm not Chunky...I'm Bhole Ram... look, it's complicated...'

Jenny looked at him incredulously. She had come there concerned for his well-being and to take care of him at a time when he was in trouble but even then he couldn't resist the chance to mock her! He just didn't...couldn't and wouldn't understand what she felt for him.

Jenny broke down crying. Poor Bhole Ram was exasperated. How on earth could he explain convincingly something that he hadn't fully comprehended himself yet? He tried anyway, for he had a kind and sensitive heart.

'Hey hey, little sister... Please don't cry...'

Jenny looked up at him and started crying some more. Bhole Ram was struggling to come up with a better way to explain himself when all of a sudden a banana landed on his face with a SPLAT!

Pintu Da, Chintamani and Uncle Geri were coming towards him angrily. Uncle Geri flew up close to Jenny and said sympathetically, 'Jenny, you go and get some rest! Some people don't deserve such kindness.'

Jenny wiped her tears and left quietly. She was quite sad. Seeing her walk away morosely made Pintu Da quite sad too, and he began singing, 'Haaaa...aaaaaaa...you bro...o...ke her heart and made her le...e...ave...you are everybody's pet peeve...'

Chintamani's shrill high-pitched voice only added to the cacophony, 'Oh what a tangled web you weave...' he cried out. Clearly, Chintamani didn't understand anything about song lyrics and poetry.

Anyway, Bhole Ram tried getting his friends to see his problem, 'Please try and understand. You all are my friends...!' Chintamani sniggered at his plea. Bhole Ram struggled with his words, 'Look, I'm in a big crisis here...please help me...I'm your friend Bhole Ram! I'm not Chunky!'

Pintu Da had had enough. He took a step towards the cage. 'Look here, don't make fun of our friend. Bhole Ram's heart is as sweet as mishti doi and your heart is as spicy as a red chili!'

'But please believe me, I am Bhole! Let me explain.' He then turned pleadingly towards Uncle Geri, 'Uncle Geri...please believe me...would I ever lie to you? Look into my eyes and tell me if I'm lying!'

Bhole Ram looked at Uncle Geri with all his earnestness and something stirred in the latter's heart. He hesitated, his heart telling him one thing and his mind the other. But then he recollected Chunky's past misdemeanours and shook his head. 'Come on let's go. It's disgusting! He has no sense of remorse...he deserves to stay locked up here with hardened criminals like Kaalia.'

Suddenly, there was a loud booming roar and Bhole Ram was hurled to the other side of the cage with the impact. He slammed into the bars and was knocked out, stunned. Kaalia pounced towards the others standing outside. Luckily for them the cage bars were strong and didn't give way. Kaalia's mighty paws tried to lash out at them through the bars but they jumped back just in time. On seeing the furious menacing panther trying to attack them through the cage bars, a frightened Chintamani dashed off in a flash.

Kaalia growled loudly, 'Enough of this talk! If you think I'm a hardened criminal, you haven't seen anything yet. Just wait till I get my claws on all of you... You will regret getting me locked here! GET OUT!'

Pintu Da wanted to correct Kaalia that they were in fact already out and it was the panthers that were locked in the cage. But he was too terrified to make any correction. Uncle Geri and he had gotten the fright of their lives and darted off. Kaalia continued glaring at them for a few more moments before retreating back to the shadow.

Uncle Geri landed on a branch above and turned back to look at the cages. He saw the monkey lying on the floor, stunned. The monkey's words were playing in his mind. Could it be true...? He thought to himself before flying off again.

Chapter 10

The hushed whispers from the shadows were the first thing Bhole Ram heard when he came to back his senses. He looked around him. Night had fallen and it seemed like all the animals and humans in the circus were asleep. The temperature had dropped considerably, making his stay in the cold steel cage even more uncomfortable. Curious about those whispers, he stealthily crept towards the grill that separated him from the panthers. Kaalia's voice rumbled and reverberated as he spoke.

'So, it's all set then?'

Bhole Ram couldn't really see through the darkness but it seemed like the panthers were having some sort of conference. The next voice he heard was Charlie's, Kaalia's trusted lieutenant.

'Yes, boss! When the maintenance man was repairing some part of the cage this evening, we stole a big steel file from his tool belt and hid it. He came back later to look for it but couldn't find it as we had hidden it well. We just need another day to file through some of these bars and then we'll be free!'

The other panthers started to cheer, but Kaalia shut them up. 'Quiet, you fools! It's not yet time to rejoice. We don't want any suspicion to be aroused, understand?'

They went silent immediately. Kaalia looked around to make sure the coast was clear. Bhole Ram had hid himself out of sight, but not out of earshot.

Thinking no one to be around, Kaalia turned back to his cronies and whispered,

'Now listen carefully, two nights from now is another circus performance...everyone will be busy with it and no one will pay attention to us. We'll escape from the cage and then surround the main circus tent. You, Charlie, will steal the flame torches kept for Chintamani's performance.'

'Aye aye, sir!' nodded Charlie.

'Once we have fire as our ally, nothing will stop us...hahahaha!'

Kaalia laughed menacingly. A horrified Bhole Ram couldn't believe what he had just heard.

Bhole Ram examined the morning. The welcome rays of the sun had dispersed some of the cold and woken everyone up. The circus was abuzz with activity. The animals went about their daily activities with a spring in their step but Bhole Ram's entire being was stooped down with the weight of woe. Here he was, locked up in a cage next to Kaalia and gang and to make matters worse, the previous night he had heard of a conspiracy to destroy the circus. If only he could get out of here and warn the others before it was too late. The sound he heard was like an answer to his prayers. The lock turned and the gate to his cage was opened.

Pintu Da was standing outside looking straight at him and singing, 'Chonky, I hope that was a lesson a lesson...a lesson for you to not play sill... yyyyy pranks anymore. You're free to goooo... ooooooo!'

So singing, Pintu Da walked off proudly. After taking a moment to register what just happened, Bhole Ram bounded out of that unhappy cage and breathing in his freedom. And then it hit him. He had a task to accomplish. He had to warn the others about Kaalia and his sinister plan. He looked around—it was of no use to try talking to Mr Gulshan simply because he wouldn't understand anything Bhole Ram would tell him. He didn't speak the animal language. Who else could he go to?

Perched high up on the branches of one of the trees, Uncle Geri was nibbling on some seeds and appeared to be ruminating. Without a doubt—Uncle Geri! Bhole Ram ran to the tree and looked up. How could he get Uncle Geri's attention? Of course, he was in a monkey's body now—he could climb up any tree he wanted. And so he did. Bhole Ram climbed all the way up to the highest branch. Uncle Geri noticed him and glared at him for a few moments before speaking, 'I hope your punishment knocked some sense into that monkey brain of yours!'

Bhole Ram stepped forward anxiously. He had to get to the point straight away.

'I have something very important to tell you.'

Uncle Geri was in no mood to indulge him

today, 'Look Chunky, I'm really not interested...'

Bhole Ram took another step forward, 'Please listen to me...it is about Kaalia. He's planning...'

His sentence was cut short rudely.

'I'm not going to fall prey to your silly pranks again. Haven't you learnt your lesson already or do you want to spend another night with those deadly panthers?'

Bhole Ram pleaded, 'Please...that's exactly what I want to talk to you about. Kaalia and his gang are conspiring to destroy the circus! Last night...'

Once again he wasn't allowed to complete his sentence. Uncle Geri had raised a wing to stop him. 'I've had enough of your tricks, Chunky!'

Bhole Ram was exasperated. This was going to be tougher than he thought. 'Please try and understand...I'm not Chunky, I'm Bhole Ram and Kaalia is seriously...'

'STOP! Enough!' An annoyed Uncle Geri flew off, as Bhole Ram looked on helplessly.

Chintamani was at his enclosure, praying earnestly

with his eyes closed, 'Dear God, tomorrow I have to perform once again in front of the audiences. P...please make sure this time that Chunky doesn't shoot any stones at my...backside.'

'This time he won't!'

Chintamani smiled. God was answering his prayers. The tap on his shoulder gave him a start and he jumped up a couple of feet before landing on his bottom. In front of him was the source of his worries, the naughty monkey himself.

'Oh, it's you! L...look Chunky, p...please don't try any tricks on me again...'

Bhole Ram tried to explain, 'I have not come to play tricks! Please listen to me...Kaalia is planning to escape and he wants to destroy...'

'No more pranks, Chunky! Please!'

How was poor Bhole Ram to explain? He took a deep breath and tried again,

'I'm not playing any pranks, Chintamani... And I'm not Chunky! I'm actually Bhole Ram in Chunky's body...'

This was too much for Chintamani's nervous disposition to handle. He freaked out and started running round in circles. Bhole Ram followed him, trying to keep up and explain himself. The lion and the monkey went round and round a few times till Chintamani couldn't handle it anymore and jumped behind a stack of hay to hide himself. Bhole Ram knew very well where he was but didn't want to make him any more nervous so he stayed put.

'Chintamani! Please...I'm not lying...'

This was the first time Chunky had called him Chintamani, and not Chintu or Chints. But still, the monkey was not to be trusted. Chintamani shouted in his shrill voice from behind the haystack.

'P-please, I implore you...leave me alone.'

Bhole Ram had to leave. There was no point in trying to talk to an anxiety-ridden lion.

Pintu Da was half-submerged in the pond, practicing his classical music when Bhole Ram ran in with urgency.

'Pintu Da...Pintu Da! Please listen to me...'

Pintu Da was shaken out of his reverie. He hated being disturbed while doing riyaaz.

'Udi Baba! Chonky! Now what?'

Bhole Ram ran up to him, panting and talking, 'Pintu Da, it's Kaalia...he is up to some trouble-making.'

Bhole Ram was interrupted once again. It was becoming quite a habit with the animals in the circus. It was like a unanimous decision that was made 'Let's all interrupt Bhole'.

'Why will anyone else trouble us? Chonky Dada, you are the expert at trouble-making!' Pintu Da wasn't interested in what this prankster had to say.

Bhole Ram was starting to get desperate, 'I'm not Chunky, I'm Bhole...'

'Quiet!' Roared Pintu Da.

Before Bhole Ram could say anything more, an irate Pintu Da tossed him out.

Bhole Ram had spent the better part of the day trying to get his friends to listen to him. The sun was slowly starting to set. He was running out of time. He climbed up the bark of a tree and, apprehensively, walked up to Jenny. Perhaps she would understand.

'Chunky! What are you doing here?' Said Jenny with a start, 'I don't want to be made fun of again.' And she turned away from him in a huff.

Bhole Ram jumped to the other side to talk to her again, 'Please listen to me. I have tried all day to speak to everyone...it's a matter of great urgency, dear little sister Jenny.'

Jenny could take it no more, 'What?! Here you go again! What is with you Chunky? Have you no remorse?'

Bhole Ram was at his wits' end, 'Please try and understand...I'm not Chunky...I'm Bhole Ram...you know that accident I had...'

You guessed it right, dear reader. He was interrupted again. This time with a resounding SLAP!

'What? What do you mean you're Bhole Ram? Do you think I'm stupid?'

Jenny started to cry. Poor Bhole Ram could have started crying himself, 'Please! I really am Bhole Ram...not Chunky...and that Kaalia...'

Jenny looked up at him, 'Oh stop it! Yes, I agree you're not Chunky! At least not the Chunky

I fell in love with... There! I said it. I had fallen in love with you! Biggest mistake of my life!'

Bhole Ram was at a loss for words. He really did feel bad for poor Jenny. What a sad way of confessing your love. A sobbing Jenny jumped from the branch and swung away. Bhole Ram had never felt more helpless. He thought to himself, 'What do I do? Is there not one animal who will believe me?'

And then it dawned on him. There was but one animal alone who would believe him.

Chapter 11

It seemed like the elephant enclosure had started to spin around. Even the stars that had appeared in the early night sky were swaying. Chunky, his mammoth body sprawled on the ground, looked at the bunch of coconuts around him. In those coconuts wasn't just coconut water, but also the fermented mixture the prankster monkey had learned to concoct from the coconuts and various other fruits. In short, Chunky was slightly tipsy! He swallowed another mouthful through his trunk.

'Dude! When I mixed this in their drinking water...instead of getting upset the animals should have thanked me! This is good stuff!'

He took another swig. This time though, it made him a bit sentimental. 'The only bad thing about being an elephant is that I don't get to see Jenny...'

He sighed deeply, and then he let out a wail, 'Jenny...Oh Jenny...! How sweet you are! I used to love getting rescued by you! You were the only one who was nice to me despite all the pranks that I played. Oh how you cared for me…'

He started getting the hiccups.

'Hic! I wish I could tell you how much I miss your boring lectures… If only I could turn back into a monkey for a few moments I would thank you and tell you that I love you!' He sat there in silence, wallowing in his sentimentality.

The familiar flutter of wings made him look up woozily. Uncle Geri who was just flying in was alarmed to see the elephant in that state, with all those coconut shells filled with fermented juice.

'Eh? What's this? Have you been drinking that awful juice?'

Chunky looked on blankly, his eyes glazed.

Uncle Geri shouted, 'Bhole Ram! Bhole Ram! What's gotten into you?'

'Hic! I don't know what's gotten into that Bhole Ram…but I do know what's gotten into me! Hic! This fantashtic drink!'

An infuriated Uncle Geri slapped him with his wings a few times. 'Snap out of this Bhole! Since when have you started drinking?'

'Hic! Shince just now!' Slurred Chunky.

He was about to take another swig when Uncle Geri toppled the coconut shell, spilling its contents on to the ground. 'You shouldn't be having all this!' He yelled.

'Don't be a party pooper!' yelled Chunky right back.

Uncle Geri tried flying closer to Chunky, who not realizing his own strength tried pushing him aside, but the strength of his trunk knocked the little old bluebird all the way over to the entrance of the enclosure.

Chunky realized what has just happened and tottered tipsily towards the entrance, muttering to himself, 'Hic! I keep forgetting how shtrong I now am now!'

Uncle Geri had fallen flat on the ground, knocked out. Chunky looked around and saw a bucket of water. He sucked in some water through his trunk and sprayed it on Uncle Geri, who woke up with a start only to see a dazed-looking elephant staring unsteadily down at him, with a silly smile plastered on his face.

'What is wrong with you? You're not the same

Bhole I know!' He said while getting up and shaking the water off himself.

Chunky nodded in agreement, 'Right you are, dear fellow! My sentiments exactly!'

There was no point discussing this any further, thought Uncle Geri while flying off and saying out aloud, 'Bhole Ram has gone mad!'

Chunky looked on confused. 'Mad? Bhole Ram has gone mad? Is that so? Shince when? Poor chap! Hic!'

He tottered back towards the tree at the other corner and plonked himself next to it. 'That Uncle Geri tweets too much... Hic!' And then Chunky passed out.

Bhole Ram screeched to a halt at the entrance. A short distance away, the big elephant was slouched under the silver fir tree, snoring away. This was going to be worse than he expected, thought Bhole to himself as he made his way towards the sleeping giant.

'Chunky! CHUNKY!' Yelled Bhole Ram, but to no avail. Determinedly, he climbed up that massive body, picking up a couple of empty coconut shells on the way and once he had scaled the summit of that giant elephant head, he let the shells drop with a big thump. His ploy worked and the giant was awake.

'Huh? What? Who?' Said Chunky, shaking his head. His quaking head shook Bhole Ram from his perch, who came tumbling down the mammoth body.

Chunky looked at the little monkey on the ground and shook his head again, 'I am me...and that guy on the ground is also me...what's going on?'

Bhole Ram stood up and shouted, 'Chunky! It's me Bhole! How can you forget what happened?'

Chunky continued to stare blankly, his thoughts still obscured in the mist of juice infused confusion. Bhole Ram picked up another coconut and threw it at his head. It was a good shot and produced the desired result.

'Uh? Oh, it's you! Now I remember. You're me and I'm you now!' Chunky burst out laughing.

Bhole Ram was annoyed. He saw all the empty shells lying around. 'Have you been drinking?'

Chunky's eyes lit up. 'Hic! Of course! Want some?'

'Chunky, this is no time for tomfoolery. I have a serious matter to discuss.'

'Go on then, I'm all ears,' said Chunky flapping his big elephant ears.

Bhole Ram jumped on his trunk to get closer to him, 'Last night, I heard Kaalia talking to his gang. They're conspiring to break out of the cage tomorrow night when the show is on. And then they plan to set the circus tent on fire and disappear into the forest! You have to do something to stop this. Please! No one else believes me!'

It took a few moments for the words to sink into Chunky's brain. And when they did, he let out some more laughter.

'Hahahahahahaha! Look at you! You're actually asking me, Chunky the Funky monkey, to save the day! I barely manage to get myself out of trouble everyday, and you expect me to fight five ferocious panthers and help everyone in the circus! Why don't you solve the problem? After all, you're Bhole Ram the Good, Bhole Ram the

Noble, Bhole Ram the Saviour!'

Bhole Ram tried his best, 'But please, Chunky—try and understand...you may be Chunky the monkey but you are now in a big elephant's body! You have the power and strength to help in this situation.'

Chunky shook his head, and Bhole fell to the ground again. 'No! I'm not risking my neck to save this bunch!'

'But I'm stuck in a little monkey's body... Those panthers will demolish me!'

Chunky leaned forward and smiled, 'Hic! My dear fellow! I don't know what else to say...'

Bhole Ram looked down at the ground. Whatever anyone might say, the fact was that he now had the body of a helpless little monkey, Chunky wasn't going to help him and the others weren't going to believe him. He was well and truly defeated.

Chunky pushed a coconut shell towards him, 'Go on! Take a swig buddy! We both have our share of troubles. Besides that panther problem, I've realized what Jenny means to me but I'm an elephant now and can't go in front of her. And you're a monkey so you can't go to meet your beloved Savitri...'

That was the sad truth. Chunky was right.

'But, Chunky, drinking this stupid juice you made is not going to make the problem go away,' said a dejected Bhole Ram.

Chunky nodded in agreement and looked down at the little monkey, 'But you know what, it tastes great and it will make you forget all this. And we both could do with a little bit of that right now.'

Bhole Ram was silent for a while. After another nudge from Chunky, he finally picked up a coconut shell and emptied its contents into his tummy.

Chapter 12

'Savitri! Ah there you are! I've been looking all over for you.'

Savitri, who was half-submerged in the stream behind the circus and lost in her thoughts, looked up to see Uncle Geri flapping his wings impatiently. His words were hurrying out of his mouth, 'What's gotten into our dear Bhole Ram? He's taken to drinking!'

Savitri couldn't believe her ears. She hastily jumped out of the stream and shook herself dry. 'My Bhole...er, I mean our Bhole Ram? Drinking? How is that possible?'

Uncle Geri twittered, 'I'm telling you! He even slapped me!'

This was hard to believe for Savitri. The sweet, gentle Bhole behaving this way? She would have to see for herself.

The sight that greeted Savitri was not something she could have ever anticipated. On reaching the elephant enclosure with Uncle Geri, what she saw made her stop in her tracks. Perched atop a reeling Chunky (whom Savitri thought to be Bhole Ram) was Bhole Ram (whom she understood to be Chunky), holding aloft a coconut shell. And they were both merrily tipsy!

Bhole Ram was chuckling, 'You know, this drink is not half as bad. And though I hate your guts... you're a fun guy after all. Hic!'

Chunky was shaking with laughter, 'Fungi? Hahaha and I used to think of you as a super bore! Well, I still do but not as much as before... Hic! Bhole, you're okay!'

Bhole Ram turned a little sentimental, 'Hic! I wish Savitri thought so too!'

Some rustling sounds diverted their attention. As if by some miracle, there appeared a not-so-slender female form just a few feet away. A dazed Bhole Ram looked on dreamily at Savitri and dropped the coconut.

'OW!' screamed out Chunky in pain.

Uncle Geri whispered into Savitri's ears, 'I need to tell everyone else how badly these two are behaving.' So saying, he flew off.

Bhole Ram excitedly jumped off his high perch

and hurried up to Savitri, who was still coming to terms with the sight before her.

'Hey there!' Shouted Bhole Ram from down below, 'Savitri... Hic! It's so see to good you...!'

He was so excited, and tipsy, that not only did he have the courage to actually speak to her but he was also jumbling his words now. Savitri obviously was a bit taken aback by the monkey's brazen behaviour. Composing herself, she looked down at the monkey.

'Thank you...good to see you too...I guess. I need to have a word with Bhole Ram.'

Chunky grinned. So she wanted a word with him, eh!

'Of course! But why just one word? You can have many words with me.'

Savitri rolled her eyes, 'Look, please excuse me... I really want to speak with Bhole Ram...I'm very hurt...'

'But that's what I'm trying to tell you! You can speak to me! And who is it that has hurt you? Just tell me and I'll fix them!'

Savitri was beginning to get annoyed with this monkey's behaviour, 'Please Chunky, I need to give Bhole Ram a piece of my mind...in private!'

In private, eh? This was getting better thought Bhole Ram. 'But why only a piece of your mind? Why don't you give me a piece of your heart as well?'

It was getting stranger for Savitri. Bhole Ram was jumping up and down animatedly now. 'Oh come on! Hic! Just a little piece of your heart...and in return I'll give you all of my heart! I'm so crazy about you!'

Savitri was completely taken aback. After a few moments of dazed silence she spoke up, 'What on earth are you talking about Chunky?'

Bhole Ram stopped jumping and put his hands on his hips. 'Look, I don't know what that Chunky's been talking about, but I sure have a lot to talk about with you... You see, sweet Savitri... I have a confession to make...'

Savitri had never been more appalled by anyone's behaviour in her entire life.

While this conversation was going on, at the other end of the enclosure another strange conversation had begun. Jenny, concerned about Chunky, had stopped by at the elephant enclosure. But she saw the monkey, whom she thought to be Chunky but who actually was Bhole Ram, in conversation with Savitri. But before she could get to him she was stopped in her tracks by the elephant, who she thought was Bhole Ram, but was actually Chunky.

I know, dear reader; this is starting to get confusing enough for us. Can you imagine how confusing this would be getting for the characters in our story?

To continue, Chunky in his stupor had completely forgotten that he was now in an elephant's body and proceeded to have the following conversation with a confused Jenny, a silly smile plastered all over his face.

'Hic! Jenny! Hello there!'

'Yes, Bhole Ram?'

Settling his bulk down in front of her, Chunky leaned over to look into Jenny's eyes with a love-struck expression.

'Why are you calling me that? You're eyes are soooo...beautiful!'

'Uh...well...thank you... You see I heard from Uncle Geri that Chunky was behaving strangely...

that he was running around telling everybody there is great danger on hand... Something about Kaalia...I need to speak with Chunky...'

'Exactly! And I need to speak to you too!'

Jenny stepped back. This was getting stranger by the minute. Why on earth was a big elephant like Bhole Ram speaking to her this way?

Chunky continued, 'You see Jenny...I've been thinking about you the last couple of days. I've never realized your worth...and I'm really sorry for troubling you so much.'

'Uh...when have you troubled me, Bhole Ram?'

Chunky glanced at Bhole Ram and then back at Jenny. 'Well, I don't know if that Bhole ever troubled you but I know I have...I have realized something...'

This behaviour was getting too much for Jenny to comprehend.

'And what is it that you have realized?'

Chunky let out a love-struck sigh and flashed his ivory smile again at Jenny.

'I have realized that I'm in love with you!'

This was probably the first time in history that an elephant had confessed his feelings for a monkey. Jenny just looked on dumbly.

At the other end, the conversation was fast heading towards the same conclusion. Bhole Ram, the monkey, looked deeply into Savitri's eyes and confessed something pretty similar.

'Savitri…I…I'm head over heels in love with you…always have been ever since I laid my eyes on you…'

It was not a normal occurrence I daresay, for a monkey to say these words to an elephant. It was Savitri's turn to be dumbfounded.

After an awkward pause of a few moments while the girls came to terms with what was being confessed to them, the reaction they had was very similar and almost simultaneous.

SLAP! SLAP!

The two horrified girls slapped their respective suitors and walked away, leaving the two boys stunned.

After an embarrassed pause, Bhole Ram, holding his cheek which was smarting with the pain of the mighty elephantine slap, was the first to speak.

'Love hurts!'

Chunky, holding a coconut shell walked up to Bhole Ram, who was still looking in the direction that the two ladies leaving the enclosure. The elephant nudged the monkey with his trunk, and gestured to the coconut shell.

'Time for some more juice, I guess!'

Chapter 13

SPLASH!
The entire bucket of icy water was emptied on Chunky and Bhole Ram.

'Huh? What? Who? Where?' Chunky woke up, his head spinning. He looked up at the sky. It was a dull, grey, cold afternoon. He had slept through the previous night and the entire morning. The sun was struggling weakly to pop its head through the clouds, but was failing miserably. The icy water though had no effect on Bhole Ram, who was still knocked out and lying only a few feet away.

Mr Gulshan, who had poured the bucket of water on their heads, looked annoyed as he walked off in a huff.

Uncle Geri, who was hovering in the air, looked at a groggy Chunky and tried knocking some sense into him, 'Bhole Ram! Mr Gulshan is very hurt and disappointed in you! He knows you've been drinking and also what you've been up to. After all he has done for us, the least we can do is to behave in a proper manner. What's gotten into you? The show begins in a few hours, your balancing act with Savitri is the opening attraction. Get up!'

Chunky scratched his head with his trunk, 'Balancing act? Isn't that what Bhole...'

Chunky stopped mid-sentence when he realized the source of the misunderstanding. No one knew of what had really happened during the lightning accident—so, Chunky had to play along since no one would believe him even if he tried to explain. And honestly, he was too woozy to even try. He just wanted to be left alone.

'Aaaah! Oh yeah...okay I remember...but hey! Could we avoid the balancing act today...I'll need some practice, dude!'

Uncle Geri hated being spoken to in that manner. 'Bhole Ram! Enough of this dude-fude nonsense! What has gotten into you since your accident? That silly Chunky is such a bad influence on you! Come on, Mr Gulshan is waiting. Get up and get going! No excuses!'

Chunky tried lifting his massive body and

standing up but he fell back on the ground in a heap.

'Uncle Geri, but...'

'No buts! Get off your butt and get ready! NOW!'

Chunky started to make another attempt to lift himself off the ground, 'Fine! But if the opening act is ruined then don't say I didn't warn you!'

He finally succeeded in standing up, and shook his head to try and clear his senses. Uncle Geri then flew up to Bhole Ram who was still slumped on the ground, fast asleep, and started flapping his wings on his cheeks in an attempt to wake up the monkey. Bhole Ram, poor fellow, unlike Chunky wasn't used to the effects of that fermented juice. He just mumbled something incoherent, turned the other way and resumed his snoring. This was hopeless, thought Uncle Geri.

'Let's leave this fool here for now! Come on, Bhole Ram.'

Uncle Geri led a still groggy Chunky out, while Bhole Ram snored away.

Lightning flashed across the early evening sky. The heavens rumbled with thunder. Angry winds were swooping down. Inside the circus tent, the crowds were fast filling up and were eagerly anticipating an entertaining evening, away from the stormy weather.

In the wing space of the stage, a reluctant Chunky was dressed in drapes and a crown, all ready for the opening act.

'Seriously! I look like a fool in these clothes. How am I ever going to balance this humongous heavy body on a rubber beach ball...?' Chunky muttered to himself.

It seemed like the crowd was in that evening for a different kind of entertainment.

The circus show was about to begin. The jokers were already on stage entertaining the audiences as they took their seats. Outside, thunder and lightning flashed incessantly across the darkening sky.

'Ladies and gentlemen, boys and girls... welcome to the Great Indian Circus!' There was a roar of applause from the happy crowd as the announcer's voice filled the big tent.

'While the storm rages on outside, we have a great show lined up for you all inside! What a great way to spend a stormy evening, in the warm, bright and colourful big tent of the Great Indian Circus with all your favourite and lovable animals!'

A huge cheer went up as both the elephants Savitri and Chunky (who everyone thought was Bhole Ram) were getting prepared. Chunky, who wasn't really ready for his debut performance as an elephant, tried leaning forward to get Savitri's attention but she was giving Chunky the silent treatment, obviously upset with his behaviour from the previous night.

And the moment Chunky was dreading finally arrived. The announcement that the opening act was to begin was greeted with a deafening applause and cheer. Chunky swallowed nervously and smiled sheepishly at Savitri, who snubbed him again. Chintamani, Pintu Da and all the others wished the two elephants all the best for their performance. Chunky, nervously, and Savitri with grace and confidence, walked on to the arena amidst rounds of applause from the excited and expectant audience.

In spite of her size, Savitri hopped on to the big rubber beach ball with practiced ease much to the delight of the audience members. Seeing her so gracefully jump on the ball, Chunky shut his eyes and said a silent prayer. He gingerly climbed on to the big ball and as he stepped on he nearly slipped. GASP! went the audience. He tried again with a struggle and this time he got on and found a semblance of balance. There was loud clapping all around as Chunky tried to move forward, but the more he tried, the more ball went out of control! He had to try hard to keep himself on the ball, which was rolling all over the arena. Savitri, who was effortlessly moving forward turned back to see why the audience was chuckling. Chunky was wobbling away, barely managing to keep himself on the ball but strangely enough not falling. It was a really funny sight and the audience, thinking it all a part of a new act burst into laughter and applause. Beads of sweat streamed down Chunky's forehead. Mr Gulshan stood there wondering what was going on as the elephant clumsily flailed and floundered his way through the act.

And then one of his forelegs slipped off the ball, followed by the other. Chunky was now balancing himself on only his two hind legs! As the ball rolled in a circle round the arena, with Chunky wobbling away on top of it, Savitri stopped to look on. She was astounded as Bhole Ram had never lost his balance and had never looked so funny while balancing himself on the ball. What on earth had gotten into him? Mr Gulshan had covered his eyes by now. He could not bring himself to watch the spectacle that was unfolding before his eyes.

The audience was delighted as Chunky, on his hind legs only, started waving his trunk about trying to maintain a balance. After going around the arena three times, Chunky rolled away on the beach ball through the exit and into the backstage area. All that the audience heard after that was a CRASH! as he fell off the ball behind the stage. There was a wave of mirth in the audience who loved this funny version of their favorite opening act! Savitri quickly bowed respectfully to the audience and hastily made her exit too.

The loud crack of thunder woke Bhole Ram with a start. He looked around him. The sky was dark, the gale was howling and the enclosure was deserted. With a throbbing head he turned and looked at the direction of the big circus tent some distance away and jumped up in a flash of anxiety. The circus show had begun and he had slept through it all! The poor animals and Mr Gulshan must have tried in vain to wake him he thought to himself. And then it hit him. His memory raced back to the conversation he had overheard the previous night. Kaalia and gang were planning their escape tonight. The circus was in grave danger! He held on to his throbbing, aching head while he processed all of this.

The streak of lightning momentarily lit up the cage, causing Kaalia's pupils to contract. As it got dark again, he gestured to his gang of panthers. It was time. They purposefully walked towards the cage bars. Charlie and the others had spent the last few hours filing the steel bars and they were finally done. With one casual swipe of his mighty paw, Kaalia snapped the already sliced cage bars. He turned to look at his gang. Another flash of lightning revealed the sinister grin on his face.

Thunder rolled in the distance as Bhole Ram ran as fast as he could through the darkness, his limbs burning as he sped towards the cages. He skidded to a halt as he reached the big panther cage. He froze with fear. The bars of the cage were cut open and it was empty.

Chapter 14

Bhole Ram's head was spinning. He was in a state of panic as he rushed through the raging winds towards the circus tent. He feared the worst. As the tent came into view, he slowed down, panting hard. Instead of cheers and applause all he could hear was screaming. He stuck his head through the flap in the canvas and what he saw terrified him. All the big lights were off and only a few dim bulbs were left on. The audience—grown-ups and little children from all the nearby towns—were running helter-skelter. Kaalia and his menacing gang had run amok inside the tent. Most of the circus animals—Savitri, Uncle Geri, Chunky, Jenny, Pintu Da and Chintamani were cowering in a corner trapped under the big safety net that was kept under the trapezes and were surrounded by three panthers. Uncle Geri hovered above his friends, completely helpless and unable to help them.

Kaalia and Charlie were on the other side circling around as the crowd fell over each other in looking for an escape. Luckily, almost all the children and adults had managed to escape without harm and the remaining few were running to safety too. It seemed like Kaalia wasn't interested in the humans. It was the circus and the animals he was after. Finally, all the humans had run out to the relative safety of the howling winds outside. It was now just the panthers on one side and the trapped animals on the other.

As quietly as he could, Bhole Ram slipped through the flap and entered the tent which was dark and eerily quiet save for the low pitched rumbling growls of the panthers. He didn't know what to do but for now he thought it would be best if he could sneak his way towards his friends, using the darkness and shadows at the edges of the tent. As he was inching his way through, all of a sudden he was yanked by Kaalia's powerful paws and flung to the corner where all the others were bunched up. Bhole Ram tumbled and landed in a heap next to his terrified friends. He looked up to see Kaalia slowly and purposefully walking towards them, a flaming torch clenched firmly between his razor sharp teeth. With one mighty jerk he flung the torch up in the air and Charlie leaped and caught it expertly between his teeth.

As Kaalia walked closer to the animals, he let out a chilling growl.

'You fools! You thought you could lock Kaalia up and not pay for it? Look how the tables turn, now it is that foolish Gulshan

and his people who are locked in those flimsy makeshift office sheds of theirs. Not only have I bolted them in there but I've also toppled those sheds over. They're now completely trapped with no way escape. As for the rest of you... Ironically, you're imprisoned by the safety net inside the same circus tent where you thought you were famous stars. Now, this very tent will become your final resting place!'

He sounded extremely serious. The terrified animals huddled closer together as Kaalia snarled again.

'I will burn this entire circus down! This tent, all the enclosures, Gulshan's offices—everything! Not a thing will remain here except ruins and ashes—this is what you get for messing with Kaalia!'

His voice echoed in the vast empty space. He glared at them and turned to walk towards Charlie and the rest of his gang. They huddled to discuss their next plan. They were only a few feet away, but probably just out of earshot.

Savitri quickly turned to Chunky and whispered, 'Bhole Ram! Please do something...

You're the only one brave and strong enough to take on these panthers!'

Chunky looked at Bhole Ram and then back at Savitri. He whispered back to her, 'Look, I don't know how to explain...but please believe me when I say this... I am not Bhole...'

Savitri cut him short, 'You have the gall to joke at a time like this? When the Circus and all of us are in such grave danger? You're not the Bhole Ram I thought you were...'

Savitri was clearly very hurt and disillusioned. So were Chintamani, Pintu Da and Uncle Geri. Chunky had to somehow convince her and the others soon—Kaalia and his gang could turn around towards them any moment. He pointed to Bhole Ram and whispered as earnestly as he could, 'That's what I'm trying to tell you. I'm not Bhole...he is!'

Tears of disappointment welled up in Savitri's eyes. 'Why are you doing this? Can't you see our lives are in danger?'

'He's right, Savitri!'

She turned to see the monkey standing close to her, just outside the net. It was all Chunky's fault she was starting to think, but the monkey had interrupted her thoughts.

Now Jenny was hurt with his behaviour too, 'Chunky! Please be serious!'

How was he to convince them? He tried his best to explain, 'Please try and believe us... I'm actually Bhole Ram! That accident we had... something happened, we both got an electric shock from the lightning and when we fell, our souls switched. I somehow came into this body, Chunky's body, and Chunky somehow went into my body. That elephant there really is Chunky! I tried telling everyone but no one would believe me...'

He looked sincerely into Savitri's eyes.

'Look into my eyes Savitri...I'm not lying...it is I, Bhole...'

They say that eyes are the windows to the soul. Savitri looked deeply into the little monkey's eyes and strangely something stirred in the depths of her heart. Her mind was convinced that all of this couldn't be true...but her heart felt otherwise. Still looking deep into Bhole Ram's eyes, she finally spoke.

'Strange as your story sounds...I believe you...'

All the others were surprised. Uncle Geri spoke up too, 'If Savitri is convinced...then perhaps...'

A loud roar interrupted the moment. Three of the panthers had set fire to the other side of the tent and the fire roared, sending a wave of unbearable heat across and lighting up the tent with a hellish glow. Collectively, the circus animals gasped in horror. Kaalia's threat was now a reality. He was still standing with Charlie just a few feet away. There was no way they could get out of this safety net and out of reach of the panthers. Kaalia looked on in evil glee as the fire erupted on the other side.

In a state of complete panic, Savitri looked at the little monkey. 'I know you're my Bhole Ram... do something...save the day...!'

It was a desperate plea for help. Bhole Ram was the only one of them who would have the courage to fight the panthers, and he was the only one not trapped inside the net. Time was running out. Kaalia and Charlie would soon set fire to their side of the tent as well.

Bhole looked at Savitri helplessly, 'But how? I'm in a little monkey's body...I have neither the strength nor power to fight them...'

'You may be stuck in a monkey's body but you have the heart of an elephant...the heart of Bhole Ram the Brave. You can take a brave heart out of a fight, but you can't take the fight out of a brave heart. Remember, Bhole...it is the heart that is important.' Savitri stared into his eyes. If Bhole Ram had to do anything, he had to do it now.

A panic-stricken Bhole Ram looked around him. The fire was rampant and spreading. Kaalia and Charlie turned towards them. Charlie had a blazing torch clenched between his teeth. On getting a signal from his boss, he flung the torch on the tent right behind where the animals were confined. The tent caught fire instantly and the animals started screaming with fear. Terror gripped Bhole Ram for the first time in his entire life. All his friends were trapped under the safety net, but he wasn't. He could get out of this alive if he wanted. Seizing his only chance in that confusion, and taking advantage of his diminutive size, Bhole Ram lifted the flap of the tent behind him and rolled under. Savitri turned to look at where Bhole Ram had been, but he was gone.

Chapter 15

The fallen leaves were flying about all over the place, as the winds had gotten even wilder and stronger. Bhole Ram ran as fast as he could away from the tent. He turned to look back at the tent as he was running away. The fire raged on. He was relieved to be away and alive, unlike his unfortunate friends. And then suddenly, he skidded to a halt. Something snapped inside of him. Here he was, running away to safety like a coward while his friends faced grave danger.

Savitri's words echoed in his head, 'You may be stuck in a monkey's body but you have the heart of an elephant...the heart of Bhole Ram the brave... Remember Bhole...it is the heart that is important...'

The angry glow of the fire some distance away cast an orange radiance on his face as realization dawned on him. He repeated Savitri's words under his breath, 'It is the heart that is important...'

Bhole Ram stood there for a few moments in

the middle of the raging storm. Slowly, but surely the look on his face transformed from that of fear to one of brave resolve.

The tentacles like flames were getting closer every second. The heat was becoming insufferable. The frightened circus animals bunched closer together and feared for their lives. The glowering flames surrounded them as Kaalia's evil laugh echoed somewhere behind. How were they going to get out of this? As if on cue and as an answer to this very question Chunky felt a forceful nudge at his leg. He looked down to see Bhole Ram, who had come back.

The monkey shouted above the roar of the fire, 'Chunky! You may be a monkey inside, but don't forget you have the body of a mighty elephant. With my heart and your strength we will save the day. It's up to us...let's do it!'

So, saying he started gnawing furiously on the net in an attempt to free them all. Savitri's heart welled with hope. Her Bhole Ram had come back to rescue them. A surge of courage passed through the animals. As soon as he got a little free, Chunky used his mighty elephant strength and tore through the rest of the net. Now freed, the animals rushed out of the corner as Bhole Ram shouted, 'Let's get these panthers and show them a thing or two about bravery!'

Kaalia and the panthers were looking on in malicious delight as the fire raged on. He turned to Charlie, 'Our work here will soon be done. We should move towards the office sheds and complete the rest of our mission before we head out for the woods...'

No sooner was Charlie about to leave than a loud voice stopped him in his tracks.

'KAALIA! GAME OVER!'

The panthers turned to see the mighty elephant emerge through the inferno; the monkey perched on top. Right behind them emerged Savitri, Jenny, Chintamani and Pintu Da. Bhole Ram was screaming, 'Savitri, Jenny and Chintamani, douse the fire! Pintu Da, you come with us...show these panthers what a tiger can really do!'

Kaalia growled, ready to take on these

domesticated animals. Just then, the heavens opened and rain they shed. Bhole Ram looked up at the sky with gratitude, 'Fate is with us now!'

The pelting rain started to slowly douse the fire. Savitri, Jenny and Chintamani ran about to save what they could of the circus.

Kaalia was livid. He wasn't going to let his plans go to naught. He roared in anger and pounced on Chunky. The other panthers followed and leaped on Chunky too. There were five panthers attacking one elephant. Chunky shook himself with all his might, dropping a couple of them off his big body. Before the two fallen panthers could leap back on the elephant, Pintu Da attacked them. He may be domesticated and lovable, but in a moment of crisis his natural instincts took over. He bravely fought both the panthers.

Kaalia caught onto Chunky's trunk and didn't let go. Charlie and the other panther were on either side of him clawing at his thick hide when there was a shrill, high-pitched roar. It was Chintamani. He looked regal, silhouetted by the diminishing flames. Just like he would during his circus act, he took one graceful leap and dug his claws into the back of the panther on Chunky's side and pulled him forcefully away. Chintamani roared, 'I am a lion... K-KING OF THE BEASTS...I th...think!'

With those words he hurled the panther, sending him crashing down a few feet away.

Bhole Ram caught a chance to get on Chunky's head. Kaalia was still latched on to Chunky's trunk and wasn't letting go. Charlie was climbing up on Chunky's back from one side. With a powerful leap Bhole Ram jumped high into the air like he would for his trapeze act and somersaulted, landing on Charlie's back and pulling him down onto the ground. Charlie tried to shake him off with all his might, but Bhole Ram wouldn't let go. He caught the fur at the back of Charlie's neck and climbed on, pulling him away from Chunky and Kaalia. As Bhole Ram was struggling with the strong panther, Pintu Da and Chintamani, who had knocked out the other panthers, came to his aid. They caught hold of Charlie's tail as Bhole Ram jumped off. With a mighty heave, they swung him round...and round, and then let go. Bhole Ram looked on with wonder as Charlie was airborne and swirling till he crash-landed in a heap at the other end of the tent, completely knocked out of his senses.

'Pintu Da and Chintamani, round up those four panthers before they can get up and throw them under the safety net!' Bhole Ram shouted instructions to the two big cats. He then turned his attention to Chunky who was still struggling with Kaalia. Savitri and Jenny were busy trying to douse what was left of the fire and save what they could of the tent.

It was just Chunky, Kaalia and Bhole Ram now. With a look of grim resolve, Bhole Ram the Brave fearlessly leaped onto Kaalia's back and dug his monkey claws into the fur at the back of the formidable panther's neck and with a great tug, yanked him off Chunky's trunk. Bhole Ram went tumbling backwards with the recoil of his own action. Kaalia quickly got back on his feet and gnarled his face as he looked at Bhole Ram tumbling away. He wasn't going to let that little monkey get away with this. He bared his fangs and was about to pounce on Bhole Ram, when Chunky's heavy foot landed on his tail, stopping him right there.

'Not so fast! No one lays a paw on my friend!'

Chunky wrapped his enormous trunk around Kaalia's body and with one mighty heave tossed him high and far, sending him crashing into the trapeze pole at the far end of the tent.

Kaalia crashed to the ground, he saw the elephant and monkey come towards him. He was hurt bad and had to get out of there. Quickly, he took a look around him. Though the rain was coming down hard, there were still some flames blazing around him. There was nowhere to run. He looked up. The only way out was up the trapeze ladder and onto the trapezes. Being a big cat, he deftly leapt on the ladder and was up in a matter of moments. Chunky and Bhole Ram looked at him expertly darting up, and on reaching up to the platform he shouted a challenge down to them, 'Climb up and catch me if you can!'

Chunky and Bhole Ram exchanged looks. Chunky narrowed his eyes and thought to himself,

'If Bhole Ram could carry his humungous elephant body up the trapeze ladder on the night of the accident, so can I today.'

Bhole Ram knew what was going on in Chunky's mind, 'You take this ladder, I'll take the one on the other side. Let's get up there and teach Kaalia a lesson he will not forget!'

Bhole Ram raced to the other ladder and expertly started scampering up towards the trapeze ladder on the opposite side. Chunky took a deep breath. This was his moment of truth to prove to himself the power of his own mind. If one was determined enough, then they could achieve the impossible. So, he set his mind to do just that.

Kaalia looked on with horror as the giant of an elephant, slowly started to pull himself up on the ladder.

'How is that even possible?' Wondered Kaalia as he witnessed the elephant making his way up.

'It is the heart that is important Kaalia... It's something you'll never understand!' Shouted Bhole Ram from the other platform, as if in response to what the panther was thinking.

Chunky was almost there. If he got up to the platform, Kaalia would have no way to escape. As Chunky heaved himself up, Kaalia bounded up onto the trapeze and swung away. Chunky looked on, panting. Kaalia's trapeze had started gaining momentum. A few more swings and he would have enough power to fling himself far off and being a cat he would know how to land on his feet. They had to act fast. Bhole Ram gripped the trapeze in front of him. Seeing him, Chunky too wrapped his trunk around his trapeze and heaved himself up. In one action, both of them jumped and swung their trapezes towards the centre. Lightning streaked across the rainy, dark sky above.

Both Chunky and Bhole Ram swung towards the trapeze in the middle that had Kaalia on it. They stretched out and tried to catch the panther as he moved out of the way just in time. Kaalia's trapeze was swinging fast and it was a matter of moments when he propelled himself off far and wide towards the entrance and made his escape. The three trapezes swung towards each other once more, and this time they got an inch closer to getting close to him but he dexterously moved away. Once again the trapezes swung away from each other.

Inside the tent, the three trapezes completed

their arc and were racing towards one another again. 'This is it,' thought Kaalia to himself. Once his trapeze reached the end of this arc, he would use the speed on the way down to propel himself. He needed to avoid getting caught just one more time. Outside the tent, a flash of lightning snaked across the sky and hit the top of the metal pole that ran through the centre of the circus tent.

Just as the three trapezes were about to converge at the centre, Chunky and Bhole Ram reached out to catch Kaalia. As they converged for that one moment, Kaalia moved out of the way by just a millimetre and Bhole Ram's paw came in contact with Chunky's trunk. At that very same moment, the current of lightning that had hit top of the circus tent pole streaked down the metal pole and sizzled Chunky and Bhole with its voltage. They were stunned and let go of the trapezes. With the residue power of the voltage, Kaalia too lost his grip.

For the second time in the last few days, time stood still for that one moment as the three animals lost their grip and fell below.

Chapter 16

A cool spray of water accompanied by the welcome sounds of birds chirping happily up in the trees was the first thing he remembered when he regained his consciousness. Bhole Ram slowly opened his eyes as he lay on the ground and the first sight that greeted him was of Savitri running to a big tub of water, filling up her trunk and running back towards him. Another spray of cool water woke him up completely. He was truly grateful to have the sweet and gentle Savitri in his life. If only he could get back to whom he was...

He tried raising his arm towards her and instead of seeing a monkey arm he saw an elephant trunk rising. Could it be...? He tried getting up and his massive body took a while to get up to its full height. He was back home in his own elephant body! He looked up at her in absolute glee and cried out happily, 'Savitri! I'm back! It's me Bhole!'

There was a loud cheer as all the circus

animals gathered around. Uncle Geri adjusted his spectacles and let out a sigh of relief, 'Finally!'

The happy sounds of cheering floated into Chunky's ears and woke him up. He was sprawled on the circus floor. When he gingerly opened his eyes and looked around he saw all the circus animals looking delighted, and Bhole and Savitri looking dreamily into each other's eyes, their trunks entwined. On seeing him stir, Jenny excitedly ran up to him.

'Chunky's awake too!'

Chunky stood up and touched his own face. He couldn't believe it! He was back to being a monkey!

'Wow! I'm Chunky the Funky monkey again!'

Jenny bounded into his arms and gave him the tightest hug she could. 'I'm so happy! I love you!'

Although a bit surprised, Chunky hugged her back tightly and shouted back with elation, 'I love me too!'

Jenny blushed as all the friends doubled over with laughter.

They were all in the circus tent, well, what was left of it. Half of it had burnt down, with most of the roof gone. Charlie and the other three panthers were tied up and bound by the safety net near the entrance. The morning sun was shining through. It was a cool, crisp, clear morning and the smell of spring wafted through the air. The accident of the previous night and the clear day signified two things—Chunky and Bhole Ram's souls had switched back into their respective bodies due to the lightning accident and that winter was finally over. Spring had arrived!

There was a low-pitched moan that emanated from only a few feet away. Kaalia, who was lying unconscious nearby, was coming to his senses. Before anyone could move in that direction, Chintamani sprang into action and bounded jauntily towards Kaalia.

'Have no fear, my friends. Chintamani the Lionheart is here! What can a mere panther do to him?' He cried out with a new-found confidence.

Kaalia looked up and bared his fangs at Chintamani who promptly leapt back in fear as all the friends had a mighty laugh at his expense. Bhole Ram and Chunky walked up to Kaalia, and Chunky tied him up hastily before he could stand up. Bhole lifted him and deposited him next to his gang. All the panthers were tied up and the circus animals felt safe.

Mr Gulshan walked in with some of his staff. Savitri and the two big cats had lifted up the office sheds and freed him and his staff the previous night. He patted all his beloved animals in gratitude for rescuing the circus and tying up the panthers.

His assistant, Sharmaji, walked up to him and enquired, 'Sir, what do we do with these ferocious panthers? Should we call the authorities?'

Mr Gulshan turned to look at the panthers and took a deep breath. He loved all the animals equally and couldn't understand why Kaalia and the others had turned against everybody.

He answered, 'No, Sharmaji. If we call the authorities then the panthers will be taken away and locked up in harsh conditions. Although we had locked them up too for the safety of the others, we still cared for them by feeding them well in the hope that our love would make them see the folly of their ways. The authorities won't treat them with the compassion all animals deserve.'

He slowly walked up to the panthers and knelt down in front of Kaalia. Sharmaji rushed to him anxiously as he didn't trust these panthers and tried to convince Mr Gulshan to step away from them, but to no heed. Instead, he affectionately petted Kaalia's head and turned to Sharmaji, 'I will never let them be taken away and treated harshly. Maybe I was wrong to lock them up in punishment,' his eyes welled up with emotion as he kept speaking, 'I've always treated them all with love, just as I would treat my own children but I guess some animals are happier being in the wild. I wouldn't want any of the animals to stay with the circus unless they wished so. Perhaps the panthers didn't want to stay here anymore...'

He stood up and looked at the majestic panthers with love. 'You know, Sharmaji...I think I know what we have to do. We must let these beautiful animals go back to their natural habitat where they belong. Perhaps they will be happier there.'

'But, sir! If they're out there in the wild they might come back and attack the circus anytime...'

Mr Gulshan knelt down again and gently put his hand on Kaalia's head. For some reason, this time Kaalia didn't growl but instead he purred and meekly looked down as if he was sorry for his actions. Through the tone of Mr Gulshan's voice he had understood his intentions and his love had won the panther over. All the other big panthers started purring as well, as if to apologize together.

Mr Gulshan looked up at Sharmaji, 'There is good and bad in all of us. What matters is what we choose to look at in others. Let's free these beautiful panthers to go back to their natural habitat. I'm sure they won't harm us anymore...I can tell from the look in Kaalia's eyes that he's sorry for his actions. He's like my child after all.'

The animals smiled warmly at Mr Gulshan's kind words.

Chapter 17

Uncle Geri looked down at the scene near the edge of the forest from one of the higher branches of the deodar tree. All the animals and staff were gathered at the edge of the Himalayan forest, and in the centre were Mr Gulshan and the five magnificent looking panthers.

Kaalia and company wished to return to their natural habitat in the forest and Mr Gulshan and the rest had come to see them off.

Uncle Geri adjusted his spectacles and smiled as he looked on at the heartwarming scene below and thought to himself, 'I guess this is what is best for all of us. The panthers willingly return to their habitat and the rest of us stay back at the circus with the loving Mr Gulshan. This way everyone is happy.'

Mr Gulshan knelt down and petted the five panthers tenderly. He wiped a tear and looked compassionately at Kaalia. 'I'm sorry to see you all go. And I want you all to know you will always have a welcoming home at the Great Indian Circus. All of us here will miss you.'

Kaalia, Charlie and the other panthers had moist eyes too as they purred affectionately at Mr Gulshan.

Kaalia walked up to the other animals and spoke to them in the animal language, 'Bhole Ram, Chunky, and all of you—I just want to apologize on behalf of all five of us. We behaved terribly and endangered all your lives. In spite of all of that, Mr Gulshan and you all have been most gracious and forgiving. Thank you from the bottom of our hearts.'

All the animals huddled around Kaalia warmly and wished him and the other panthers all the best for their new beginnings in the forest.

'Thank you for helping Mr Gulshan and all of us to restore the circus to its glory. In fact it looks even better now! Please come by and say hello to us often,' said Bhole Ram.

'Bye-Byeeeeeeee and see you soooo-ooon!' sang out Pintu Da.

Kaalia nodded and smiled. He then turned to look at Chintamani, who got nervous and stepped back.

'Uh...K-Kaalia...I hope you won't attack us anytime soon...I mean...you're going to be close by in the forest so...'

Kaalia smiled sincerely, 'I'll never attack you, my friend...or any of you for that matter. I've realized that you all are my family and it was my mistake to think otherwise. In fact, since we'll always be close by in the forest, we'll make sure no animal ever dares to attack the circus and if they do, they will have to face five angry panthers that will do everything they can to protect their friends here. I'll see you all soon...this time to say hello!'

A loud cheer went up. Kaalia and the others turned and made their way into the forest. Just before they walked into the tree line, Kaalia looked back once more at all his friends. The five panthers then walked into their new home in the forest.

Uncle Geri looked up at the morning sky. It was a clear blue and the entire valley was bathed in the warmth of the sun. The flowers had started to bloom and there was a riot of colour all around. The animals started to make their way back to the circus.

Uncle Geri thought to himself, 'The last few

days had been very hard on all the animals in the circus. And yesterday was especially rough. But there's a lesson in it for all of us…a lesson we should never forget.'

The wise old bluebird took a deep breath and with one practiced leap he soared into the air and off he flew to join his friends.

'And what lesson is that?' You might ask, dear reader.

However dark and stormy the winter may be, remember one thing—winter always turns to spring!

Acknowledgements

I would like to thank my family: my mother, my wife Jasmine and my brother Sunil for their valuable feedback, support and encouragement throughout the process of writing this book.

A big thanks to filmmaker, author and my neighbour Jyotin Goel. Reading his books for children inspired me to write one too. I would also like to acknowledge his very useful guidance and feedback during the writing process.

Many thanks to Vijash Kothari of KWAN who sent my manuscript to Rupa Publications, and to Shambhu Sahu for finding my manuscript good enough to be a part of Rupa Publications and all his support and guidance up until it became a book.